A BOX FULL
OF DARKNESS

A Box Full of Darkness

by

Simon Avery

This book is for my Dad, who opened the
door to books and films and Scott Walker.
I miss you.

~ 1 ~

Trelawney was momentarily light-headed. He swayed in the narrow corridor between the book cases, and felt the ground rushing to meet him before an old man reached out a steadying hand. His grip was surprisingly firm. He had Trelawney before any harm was done.

"*Steady* there," the old man said. Once he was sure Trelawney was balanced again, he relinquished him. "The floors are uneven," he observed. "The old buildings are always like this." He pressed his shoe into the threadbare carpet; the floorboards screeching like an animal in pain. "Makes you feel bloody seasick, doesn't it?"

He had a dog with him, a large, shabby-looking wolfhound. With his feet firmly planted again, Trelawney offered it the back of his hand to sniff. Satisfied, it slumped heavily to the floor. Trelawney recognised both man and dog. They were staying at the same hostel in Ambleside, at the northern tip of the lake. Each morning, Trelawney had noticed the dog trailing slowly after the old man, into the lift and then across to the terrace for breakfast.

Trelawney had begun every day of his holiday in the lakes by walking down from the hostel to the water's edge with his flask of tea. There was a bench where he could sit and attempt to arrange or arrest his thoughts, scattered as they'd become. He'd taken his three weeks of holiday allowance all at once this year, consumed with a sudden and fervent desire to leave London and visit Cumbria, where he hoped the air would revive something that had lain dormant within him for the past few years. He'd taken a cheap single room with a shared bathroom. He'd had to save for several months.

At the water's edge Trelawney would watch the morning sun rising above the fells, the slopes lifting themselves to the light; softer, almost infinite gradients of colour revealing themselves as he sipped at his tea. The gentle lapping sound of the water and the hiss of the breeze through the trees stacked up behind the hostel. Gulls twisting on the gentle air currents above him, crying out. All of these things carried with them the gently thrilling emergency of the present. Day by day, he'd felt a calm settling into his bones, a stillness replacing that initial fluttering absence at the edge of his consciousness.

The old man had a similar ritual to Trelawney and, after breakfast, would venture down from the terrace to sit on one of the neighbouring benches beside the water. Trelawney hadn't formed much of an opinion on him, other than noting his enormous dog and the large bag he carried around with him, the like of which Trelawney recalled general practitioners using when they made house calls. He would doff his cap at Trelawney and thus far that had been the extent of their interaction.

This morning there was a fine rain in Ambleside, clinging to the tourists in their Barbour jackets and walking boots. Everyone had shuffled into cafes for an early lunch to escape the weather. Trelawney had instead allowed himself to be tempted inside the warren of back rooms of a second-hand bookshop, and then into a sudden hot flush that had almost taken his legs out from under him, if not for the other man.

The old man's mackintosh was stained and ripped and the hems of his trousers were uneven, displaying one bare ankle. He lowered his wire-rimmed spectacles to the edge of his nose and squinted at Trelawney, his teeth gritted. "Sheltering from the rain?" He didn't wait for answer. "You have to expect it in the Lake District, more often than not."

Trelawney nodded and shifted his attention to the rows of books. Narrow paths with threadbare carpet led him deeper into the shop, the rooms lit with bare 40-watt lightbulbs, covered in cobwebs. He considered a set of faded orange Penguin books lined up across a grey tiled mantelpiece. There was soot in the hearth. A grimy looking kitchen was set to one side with a kettle, some chipped mugs, a kettle and a small sink.

"Do you live locally?"

Trelawney hadn't heard the man approach. The dog trailed after him, circled a spot in the centre of the room and collapsed again.

Trelawney had begun to nod and then recognised his error. "No, I'm on holiday," he said. "I live in London. More's the pity."

"Costello," the man said, offering his hand.

"Trelawney." They shook hands stiffly. There was something else behind Costello's flinty gaze, but Trelawney couldn't decide what it was. He couldn't place his age either. Anywhere from 55 to 75. "Are you a tourist too?"

Costello laughed. "No. I used to work in the area. I'm in-between gainful employment at present." After a moment he added, "No fixed abode."

Despite his circumstances, Trelawney couldn't escape the notion that there was a heft to the man's bearing, a certainty that he felt he lacked. But just lately the conviction that something was missing from his life had seemed to dog him.

There was a gap in his memory. Around this lacuna the recollections he did have were quite unnaturally precise: the absolute clarity of sitting in a field of lavender in Evesham one afternoon some years ago. There had been a sudden rain shower, but then the sun had emerged. The trees were dripping with rain;

the birds were singing again. He could hear the low industrious hum of bees in the lavender. Two men were calling out to each other on the towpath nearby. The moment was rich with imminence; something, he felt sure, would emerge from this expectant moment. A revelation of some kind. And, bookending this memory, a wretched low point: sitting alone in the room he'd rented from a young professional couple who owned a narrow but perfectly formed house in Putney. The husband was a minor film director who wore clothes from charity shops and who would talk in furiously intense bursts at Trelawney and then pause and stare intently at him as if expecting something of substance in return. The wife was a teacher at a dance school on the high street, leading a parade of stiff little girls in arabesques. Trelawney had listened to them arguing and then fucking while he sat beside a three-bar fire that smelled of burning dust, with his books arranged on the window ledge, and a shopping channel muted on his little TV, the feeling of utter desolation growing in him like cancer. It was like someone had snipped an article from a newspaper and left everything else intact around it. A box full of darkness. This blank space fluttered sometimes in Trelawney's mind, suggesting some cognitive leap that remained frustratingly elusive. The ghost of everything he'd once owned and known, just out of reach.

And still it fluttered.

Trelawney noticed the large black Gladstone portmanteau bag with its brass lock and fittings.

"Were you a GP?" he asked, nodding towards the bag.

"In another life," Costello said. "A medical negligence suit saw to that." He stepped closer and whispered, although there was no one else back here. "I diagnosed a man with acute gastritis and prescribed him with painkillers and antacids. Three days later he was in intensive care with septicaemia and toxic shock syndrome. Died not long after."

"Oh. I'm sorry. That must have been awful."

"Hmm. I suppose it was." Costello glanced about and then said: "Memoriae?"

Trelawney withdrew, bewildered. "I'm sorry, what?"

"You know," Costello said. "*You know.* That's the real reason you're here, isn't it? I mean, that ridiculous charade with the fainting into my arms..."

Trelawney attempted to laugh off this moment of irrational behaviour. "I'm afraid I have no idea what you're talking about."

"Would you like to know what's in my bag?"

Trelawney thought he could detect the smell of alcohol on the man's breath. "Not especially, no."

"But you *feel* it, don't you? I can tell. *Weightless*. Like a dandelion seed, dancing on the breeze, you are. It's a common symptom."

"Look, I suppose I should be going," Trelawney said, feeling some sense of implied threat in the old man's words. And something else besides.

"I suspect that you envy them, don't you, the people out there?" Costello said, placing a firm hand on Trelawney's shoulder. He waved at the window, which only afforded them a view of another building, the back of a cafe of some sort. The rain was still coming down. "Those people with their lives: queuing in Tesco; sitting in traffic jams; playing with their kids; that week on a beach, or beside the pool in Tenerife." Costello shrugged. "They *know* their lives. They *understand* how they got here from there. Do you see what I mean? Tell me if I'm boring you."

"I'm afraid I don't really know what you're getting at..." Trelawney began, but he did, and it made him hesitate long enough for Costello to realise that he was correct.

"They took something from you, didn't they? Something vital. Sizeable."

"Who?"

"*Memoriae*, man, Memoriae! For Christ's sake, keep up," Costello hissed. "When you have part of your narrative removed, where does it leave you? I'll tell you: fucking *rudderless*, that's where. Lines on your face that you feel you haven't earned, huge reservoirs of emotion like cul-de-sacs in your mind. There's no foundation to build anything new, anything of real substance on. I'm right, aren't I?" Trelawney simply stared at Costello, very aware of how directionless he'd felt these last few years. As if he'd been dropped into a life which was not wholly his own.

"Why don't we find a cafe?" Costello suggested in a kinder voice. He took Trelawney's arm to guide him back through the labyrinth. "Look, the rain is stopping, and I could absolutely murder a latte."

2

The clouds slipped behind the fells and then the sun emerged, coaxing the tourists, with their bellies full, back out onto the streets. Trelawney and Costello escaped the crowded streets in Ambleside and took the bus back to Lake Windermere. They found a cafe with a pretty terrace near Waterhead pier. There were boats lined up on the shore, speckled with rain, ferries filled with tourists, coming and going. Costello's dog sat beneath the wet table and quickly fell asleep, snoring loudly. Their drinks arrived. Costello's latte had a ridiculous foam of cream on it. They sat for a while in silence, Trelawney feeling as if he was on the precipice of something that he had no real desire to discover, but which was an absolute necessity to know. A couple of women in life jackets took a catamaran out onto the water. It was as still as a mirror. The vastness of the view was still something Trelawney was becoming accustomed to; in London it was all tube stations and Oxford Circus; people everywhere. The solemn, beautiful tapestry of the Cumbrian countryside seemed to call out to something deep within him; it felt like a return to a rustic permanence he thought he'd once known, but felt, when he searched his memory, that he had not. A subtle alchemy of landscape that suggested freedom and release from all the doubts and concerns that had clouded the last few years of his life.

"I don't know you," Costello said after a while. There was a ridiculous moustache of cream on his top lip, which he was either oblivious to or simply didn't give a shit about. "Let's be perfectly clear about that. But I know your circumstance. I recognise the look by now."

"And what look is that?" Trelawney said.

"Lost. Absent from your own life. You're a stranger to yourself."

"That seems like a lot for a total stranger to see."

"But I'm correct, aren't I?"

Trelawney stared at the old man, aware that his hands were bunching into fists. He didn't enjoy having his life so quickly and completely apprehended. It irritated him.

"That part of your past, the one you're mourning whether you know it or not – it's gone, I'm afraid. I don't believe I have it."

"*You don't believe you have it?* What the devil does that mean?"

Costello shrugged and ran his hand into his dog's thick, wet fur. The portmanteau bag was still at his side, firmly closed. "I apologise for being so vague. I had to be sure you were one of their out-patients."

"Who?" Trelawney said. "Who are *they*? Who are *you*?"

"I used to work for them. The company that did this to you."

"What did they do?"

"Well. Where to begin? They filleted you of part of your life. Harvested it. I assume you have a scar."

Trelawney felt a sudden vertigo, as if he was slipping from this world into one he was ill-prepared for. The ugly puckered scar that ran from his belly to his groin. He had no memory of the operation that had necessitated it.

"How do you know about that?"

"The scar? If you handed them money then you have the scar to prove it." Costello leaned forward. "What about your dreams? Have you dreamed about it yet?"

"Dreamed about what?"

"Let's not play silly buggers. *The void.* Tell me about the dream."

Trelawney sighed at Costello and then looked away, at the women out on the lake, at the light, shifting and lapsing, the sound of the water washing across the shoreline, settling into his bones, an existential peace that seemed tantalisingly out of reach. "There isn't much to tell," he said finally. "I'm lying in darkness. Something is growing around me, like black moss. I can feel it growing inside me too. Little shoots bursting from my pores, popping up across my skin." He paused, aware that his heart was racing. "It feels like I'm close to the night sky, like I could touch it if I could just reach up. It's very clear, like it is out here, with no light pollution. Millions of stars, the moon, a faint band of light stretching from horizon to horizon."

"And?"

"And then there's a deeper blackness, sweeping across the sky. A..." He hesitated to say it. "A void, like you say, swallowing the stars, blotting it out, replacing it with nothing."

"And?"

"There's nothing else. I wake up."

Costello nodded. "I see."

"Yes, but that's just it. I *don't*. I don't see how any of this should mean something to you."

"And yet it does."

"What's in the bag?" Trelawney asked.

"This?" Costello said and glanced down. "This is my casual atrocity bag." He got to his feet. The dog stirred from his slumber and, after a moment's concerted effort, lifted himself too.

"Where are you going?"

Costello waved a hand dismissively. "I have to see my wife. I left my car in town so I'll have to catch a bus. I mustn't be late."

"I'm sure she wouldn't mind. You must have more to tell me."

"Not today, I'm afraid. She's in a care home. She expects me at specific times. Dementia, you see."

"I'm sorry."

"Give me your number," Costello said. "I'll take you somewhere. It might unlock something. It might not. No promises."

Trelawney wrote his mobile number on a napkin. Costello took it without another word. A bus had just begun to pull away. Costello chased it down, cursing the driver until he stopped. The dog lumbered after him, clambered onto the bus, and then they were gone.

3

The following day, Trelawney found himself on a train to Ulverston, a pretty little town in the south of Cumbria. There was a market on in the centre; men and women selling brightly coloured jewellery and heavily colour-saturated photographs, locally produced cheese and pies. There was bunting hanging across the narrow little streets. The gentle murmur of conversation from the stall owners and tourists sitting outside cafes. Rain in the air again, soaking everything in time. Trelawney was distracted by it for a while but then allowed geography to steer him out of the town and down lanes which were hemmed in on either side by narrow grey or whitewashed houses. He arrived at a wide junction with traffic on four sides. He had no idea where he was going, but it felt curiously like his feet had led him this way hundreds, if not thousands of times before. They were aching by the time he fetched up on the corner of a narrow road of council houses. There were cars parked all the way down the street, making the traffic wait as a bus lumbered up the slope. A taxi was idling, waiting for someone. A man, covered in plaster dust, was loading junk into a skip. Trelawney didn't know what he was looking for, but there was a curious electricity in his extremities here, as if the area was charged with some kind of latent mystery that only he could solve. He looked at each of the houses, attempting to kindle something in his memory, but it remained frustratingly elusive. He walked up and down the street, half expecting someone to open their door and recognise him, or else call the police. By the time he was at the bottom of the lane, he knew that there would be a post office on the corner and a garage on the opposite side. He was gripped with déjà vu. The rain became almost torrential. It beaded in Trelawney's hair. He considered going into the post office for shelter, and to see if someone found him familiar, but instead he dithered outside, appalled at his own diffidence. Soon he was soaked to the skin. This town seemed so familiar to him, and yet utterly foreign. There was meaning here, but he had no way of translating it into something tangible. For that he supposed he'd need Costello.

Eventually, obscurely disappointed in himself at not being able to pierce a hole in the world he might once have known, Trelawney made his way back up the hill to the station, to catch his train back to the hostel.

~ 4 ~

Costello had a shabby old Fiat 500. He sat hunched over the steering wheel with a look of incandescent determination on his face. He was road rage waiting to happen. He hurtled down curving back roads at seventy, quickly dropping down the gear column and braking hard as corners slid into view. It was so cramped inside it was absurd. Trelawney had his legs pressed uncomfortably into the muddy footwell; he found himself involuntarily jabbing his foot on imaginary brake pedals, as if that might save him from an imminent fiery death. The dog took up the entirety of the back seat, the car smelling of the animal's seemingly permanently wet fur.

Costello drove them north, through Ulverston and onto the A592 through the Kirkstone Pass, towards Ullswater. The sun had risen early today; by now the heat was thick and exhausting. The sun was spiking off the windscreen; it slanted through the trees and glittered on vast expanses of water that appeared like little miracles to Trelawney's eyes. Costello was inured to the casual beauty of the landscape; he barely spoke or even glanced across when the view was filled with something that Trelawney found quite glorious.

Without warning, Costello pulled into a lay-by on the A66 near Castlerigg. Trelawney had seen signposts for a stone circle nearby, out beyond the drystone walls and across an endless patchwork of fields. He listened to the engine ticking in the silence, the dog panting on the back seat.

"Where are we?" Trelawney asked.

Costello sniffed, shrugged. "It's not important." He looked older today, Trelawney thought, more worn. It looked like he hadn't shaved, and his skull was mottled with small, flat, dark blemishes. His hands were still bunched around the steering wheel. He peered over it, up at the sky, a pinched look on his face. "Come on," he said. "We're going for a walk."

The dog didn't need a lead. It lumbered after the two men, its head lolling from side to side, panting heavily. Costello led Trelawney over a drystone wall and across a field, then over a well-worn stile. Sheep shit everywhere; by the time they reached their destination the tread of Trelawney's boots was compacted with it. Down below them a private road snaked towards a large manor house in the distance.

"Woodholme Manor. See it?" Costello said, letting a gnarled tree take his weight while he jabbed at the shit on his shoes with a stick.

"Yes, I see it." Trelawney was growing impatient. He blotted the back of his neck with a handkerchief. "Is this pertinent to what happened to me?"

"Of course it is. I'm not chauffeuring you around for my sodding health, am I?"

It looked like a country club, or a 5-star luxury hotel where comfortably well-off couples might take a weekend break. Heavily forested grounds that stretched for miles in all directions.

"Memoriae."

"Memoriae?"

"That's what they're called."

Trelawney nodded. "Why couldn't we just walk along the lane to the gates?"

"Don't be a fucking imbecile! There are cameras everywhere."

"Can they explain what happened to me?"

Costello laughed bitterly. "They could but they won't."

"If I was a patient, then surely there would be records."

"There are. I found your contract."

"My contract?"

"A standard disclaimer and a consent for surgery and procedures. 'I understand the risks of anaesthesia or sedation, risks and hazards, no guarantee or assurance has been given by anyone as to the results that may be obtained,' etc, etc."

"How do you have that?"

"Someone I know hacked into Memoriae's intranet through the use of web-browsers. They accessed their payroll systems, patient documentation and the like. It didn't take long to find yours. If you like I can show it to you later."

The memory of the manor house seemed to lie beneath some blurred detachment in Trelawney's mind, a wall that he couldn't decide how to scale. The longer he stared at it, waiting for some sign of life, the more this curious loss of equilibrium persisted. A circumscribed world, gently taunting him with its very existence. "Who are they?"

"At some point in your past you decided you needed to forget something, or most likely some*one*," Costello said. He sat down heavily on a rock, the air going out of him. The dog slumped down beside him. "They started out with fairly beneficent intentions: PTSD, substance use and psychiatric disorders. Victims of violent crime or other traumatic events. But a lot of people have very prosaic reasons for wanting to forget."

"And they, what, remove those harmful memories?"

Costello nodded. "Selective memory erasure."

"But surely that's impossible."

"There are various advances being made with drugs that, when applied to certain areas of the brain, usually the amygdala, have some success in being able to erase memories. Tracing and destroying neutrons, erasing target memories."

"And this is what Memoriae do?"

"In a roundabout fashion, yes."

Trelawney glanced across the fields towards the house again and in his memory glimpsed an elegant Georgian room with carved statuary depicting Roman gods and goddesses, griffins, satyrs. An almost overwhelming stillness, a silence, a winding staircase... It was there, then occluded again, like clouds passing over the sun.

"Several hours before your procedure you ingest something. I'm not entirely sure what it consists of or what its exact effects are, but after a day or so, it grows inside the body, isolating during hypnosis these emotional memories for different aspects of information. It's a sort of Neuro-Linguistic Programming that's based on the premise that memories are stored in a linear pattern. The next few steps are unclear. It's a vague, nebulous process. I suspect but cannot prove that there's an aspect of ritual about it."

Trelawney simply stared at the old man, speechless.

"After a couple of days the substance you ingested has grown sufficiently, pinpointing the specific memories that the patient wants excised. Then they simply cut the offending memories from the body."

"They *cut the memories* out of you?"

"We should get back to the car," Costello said, getting to his feet again. "I think it's time to show you what's in my casual atrocity bag."

Costello opened the boot and lifted the portmanteau bag out. "This," he said, sliding a small key into the brass lock, "contains some of the memories that Memoriae have removed from people in the last year or so." He unclasped the bag and pushed it open. Trelawney stood at the edge of the lay-by behind Costello's Fiat, with the sickly sweet smell of meadowsweet invading the back of his throat. The trees, green and tangled above them. The sun at its zenith in the sky. Insects roaring in the fields. The tarmac looked wet; the horizon glimmered in the distance. Trelawney couldn't see the manor house from here. It had already taken on the quality of a hallucination. There was simply too much to process.

The first few items Costello withdrew looked innocuous enough and didn't especially validate any of his fantastic claims. A handful of black husks of sunflowers, the petals flaking away in his fingers; a geometric stone that seemed to click and unfold beneath the weight of his fingers, like a Chinese puzzle box; a bone carving of what looked like a foetus with thorns embedded in its surface; some shells that seemed to spiral so far inwards that you felt you were falling into them. Costello lifted each of them from the bag, showed Trelawney and then displayed each of them in turn on the parcel shelf of the Fiat as if they were precious museum pieces.

"Handle them," Costello said. "You'll see."

Trelawney picked one up and the memory unfolded like origami in his hands:

A wet weekend in Newquay, where a girl of 14 loses her virginity to a man much older than her. She falls pregnant and has an abortion.

And another:

A sunny afternoon in London. A man and his wife stand on the platform at Belsize Park, waiting for the train to arrive. They are perfectly happy. Then the man's wife turns to him and says I can't go on anymore with this life and leaps onto the tracks a moment before the train arrives at the station. It kills her instantly.

Another:

A boy joins the Army at the age of 16 to get out of his home town, Barrow-in-Furness, after years of homophobic bullying. He becomes an electronic warfare specialist in the Royal Signals and defuses 93 bombs in Afghanistan. Out of an 11-strong team he is the only one to return home unharmed. He wakes up most nights seeing his friends bodies blown into tiny pieces or charred black like something from Pompeii.

There were more but Trelawney was already overwhelmed.

"These are relatively fresh," Costello said, taking the memories back and placing them into the portmanteau bag. Trelawney could still see them. Deep within their folds, the stories. Angle your head slightly and you could see something else, some hitherto unseen facet. "After a few years they eventually degrade naturally."

"How do you have these?" Trelawney asked. The memories were still humming on his skin, a resonance in the back of the mind, like being flooded with thousands of images all at once. It was too much.

"I was an employee for Memoriae for twelve years after the malpractice suit. Among other things I was tasked with disposal of the erased memories. They're generally incinerated as medical waste, just like amputated limbs." Costello locked his casual atrocity bag and placed it back in the boot.

"But you kept these. Stole them."

"I did. My contract was terminated last year."

"Do you have mine?" Trelawney asked finally. "My erased memories?"

"I'm not entirely sure. I have another bag filled with them, but it's in storage."

"I think I lived here," Trelawney said after a moment of surrender to the idea. "Not actually here. Ulverston. Before the memory was removed." Saying it aloud was like confirmation, and acceptance of all the ambiguities of this old man's story.

"It's certainly possible." Costello closed the boot and leaned against the Fiat. "It's not a wholly precise method. There are, of course, extant records of births, deaths, marriages. Employer records. These can't be erased from a person's life unless they have sufficient funds. So you could certainly walk down your old street and bump into the abusive ex-husband whom you paid to forget."

There were other aspects to the procedure. Costello explained them as they drove back to Windermere. These details, he said, increased the efficacy of the treatment in the long term. A psychologist would assess a patient's mental state going forward, and before the procedure they would be assigned an aftercare director who would work with them to ensure that after their memory was excised they didn't simply go back to the old part of their life which they'd paid to forget. Relocation was sometimes necessary: a new job, a new home in a new town. Memoriae claimed to perform an MRI afterwards to determine if there had been any noticeable damage to the hippocampus, although Costello contested this. Someone would transport the patient afterwards so they could make a clean break and begin their new lives in earnest. "But there's contextual memory," Costello noted. "*Instinct*, yes? Pathways to memories that are reactivated by retrieval cues at the actual sites of events. The mind is a remarkable encoding and storage system."

Costello dropped Trelawney off at Ambleside Pier. He claimed to have moved on from the hostel and was staying at a friend's flat in Penrith. They sat with the car idling while Costello took Trelawney's email address. He promised to send him a link to a website. Before he got out, Trelawney said, "Your wife. You said she has dementia?"

Costello nodded. "Yes, she's in a care home."

"Was she a patient? At Memoriae?"

Costello stared out of the windscreen emptily for a moment. "Yes," he said.

"What was she trying to forget?"

"Let's not be coy, Trelawney," Costello said. "It doesn't suit you. Don't *you* wish you'd never met me?" He put the Fiat into gear and drove away.

~ 6 ~

A link was waiting in Trelawney's inbox by the time he got back to the hostel after dinner. His phone wasn't particularly new but he had some mobile data that he could use to bring up the website link to look at. It was an amateurish blog. The posts seemed to have been written by several different people, detailing the business practices of companies like Memoriae. There was a prevalent air of paranoia and conspiracy that marred anything with any trace of veracity. Trelawney recognised Costello's posts immediately, but they covered much of the same ground as their conversation today. A selection of photographs of objects purporting to be excised memories, along with descriptions of their details. They were like classified ads, or lost animals, waiting to be discovered by their owners. There were photos of the interior of the manor house along with detailed blueprints of the layout of the building. Trelawney studied them for a while, expecting some spark in his memory but there was nothing. Most of the posts petered out after paragraphs of repetition and speculation. There were several essays drawing attention to the link between memory erasure and early onset dementia, and the lack of legal recourse when there was a clear correlation to be inferred.

After a while, tired from the days' exertions, Trelawney went to bed and slept soundly. He dreamed of finding his personal effects at the back of a particularly dusty junk shop in Ulverston. There was nothing of great value to speak of, nothing that suggested a man of great significance. A rail of clothes, from the child to the man; several piles of his favourite books; a selection of furniture; a box stuffed with correspondence and postcards from a different era; albums filled with photos of his departed parents... Trelawney lingered here and there, found himself clambering over tables and chairs, tunnelling deeper and deeper into the darkness of the store. Finally, stumbling between a single bed that he'd slept in as a child and a box filled with old teddy bears, he discovered a door that led deep into blackness. Here Trelawney discovered himself lying in what looked like black moss, his eyes fixed on the inky blackness stealing across the great arc of sky above him. His heart began to thunder as the darkness convulsed around him and his memories began to grow, like malignant spores inside his body.

~ 7 ~

Near the end of his stay Trelawney visited Ulverston again. He alighted at the station with his palms soaked and the breath frozen in his chest, wholly unsure of himself, of his needs at this point. He was aware of the precarious nature of his situation. He kept going over his conversations with Costello, considering the wildness in the man's eyes. He couldn't resolve any of the things he'd told him in his mind. As ludicrous as his claims were, there remained some flicker of credence in Trelawney's mind.

The flood of contextual memory, surging to the surface when he lingered in the streets of this town, seemed like proof, of a kind. When he searched his memory, he had no recollection of Ulverston, but as soon as he found himself meandering through the pretty little streets, he felt a familiarity, a sense of a life having been lived here.

The sun was out again, and the cobbled streets in the centre of town were filled with tourists, crowding the cafes and charity shops. He made his way to the Laurel and Hardy museum at the edge of town and spent an hour in there, losing himself in something unequivocal that he'd loved once, those old films they'd played on BBC2 when he was a child. But it was not his childhood that was in doubt. He had firm memories of that time, and, after having sat down at the edge of the lake one evening with his flask of tea, had attempted to map out the course of his life as he recalled it. He could account for the first thirty-two years, and then he was left with a twenty-year gap, a vast continent of unremembered territory. He made a diagram, a flow chart of events, of childhood and university and girlfriends and learning to drive, working in Manchester and Morecambe and the Midlands, spending a month in hospital after a car accident on the M6. And everything afterwards: the reduced circumstances of that rented room in Putney and the menial work he was engaged in. It didn't seem like enough. A man in his fifties, washed ashore from twenty years at sea, or wherever he'd been in all that time. No friends from before, no living relatives, no family of his own. He'd discovered an official website for Memoriae but there was very little to go on. It advertised itself as an exclusive health clinic with a focus on memory and the mind, boasting luxurious amenities and state of the art facilities, internationally renowned consultants and '...exceptional levels of discretion and care.' There was an email address provided for prospective clients. Trelawney sent them a message, asking outright if he had ever been a patient at Memoriae's facility in Casterigg. Thus far no one had responded to his email.

He didn't find whatever it was he thought he might in the streets around Ulverston, but every corner he turned seemed to promise the truth of things. He returned to the narrow road from his last visit and walked up and down its length until he was aware he was drawing attention to himself. He felt he was constantly on the precipice of peeling away the skin that had grown over that part of his life and uncovering the truth of it all. It would happen in a moment, he felt certain. One thing would fall into place and then everything else would follow, like dominoes.

But the day grew long and his feet got sore. He reluctantly yielded to the desolate streets. All the disturbed atoms of that former life resettling in the air around him. Trelawney made his way back to the station and sat on the platform, staring emptily into space. For a while there was no one else waiting, but after fifteen minutes a woman emerged from the darkness of the ticket office and, with nowhere else to lay down her holdall and sit, she placed herself beside Trelawney and exhaled. Her boots were well-worn, mud all down one side of her jeans and her Berghaus coat. She gathered her thick hair into a scrunchie and tied it up on top of her head.

"Long day?" Trelawney said, companionably.

"Like you wouldn't believe!" she said, laughing. She had a thick Yorkshire accent.

"Went arse over tit on the way down the Old Man of Coniston. Sorry if you can smell me but I'm probably covered in sheep shit."

Trelawney sniffed. "I think it's just mud. Are you on your own?"

"Ha!" she said, loudly. "If you asked my ex-husband, he'd certainly say so."

"It's like that, is it?"

"Yes, I'm afraid it is," she said, trying to stuff a badly folded Ordnance Survey map into her holdall. "Why do these buggering things never fold back up properly?"

"Have you tried Google maps?"

"It's not the *same*," she said brightly, mock punching his knee. She had an amiable manner, but Trelawney thought he could detect brief flashes of vulnerability behind her watery blue eyes. She quickly masked it with a wide smile. "My name's Georgina, by the way," she said.

The light was fading now and still there was no sign of the train. "Trelawney," he said and offered his hand.

"Is that the whole name or what? Have you come straight from Hogwarts?"

Trelawney laughed. It sounded unfamiliar to him, like a vestige of his former, lost life. The box opening, just a touch, letting a glimmer of light in. He could feel the tension going out of him, as if life was reaffirming its control on a universe that had been subtly tampered with. He thought for a breathless moment that the world was reordering itself around her smile.

"My name's Dennis," he said.

"It's a pleasure to meet you, Dennis. Now would you like to see some pictures of my pet duck?"

He laughed again. They were catching the same train. They talked all the way back.

~ 8 ~

There was a parcel waiting for Trelawney when he arrived back at the hostel. He took it up to his room and placed it on the bed. There was a note attached.

> *I found this in one of my casual atrocity bags. But don't cling to it. Everything is impermanent. Embrace the exquisite present! Before you know it, everything is beginning again.*
> *C.*

Trelawney peeled the tape from the box and lifted the flaps, then hesitated. After some further deliberation he closed it up again and left it on the side table. Before he got into bed he contemplated the box several times. Exhaustion finally consumed him and he fell asleep.

In the morning, he woke, gripped with the absolute necessity to know what was in the box. He put his hand in and withdrew the object. It was a tin kaleidoscope toy. It was brightly coloured but rusted at the ends. Trelawney vaguely recalled having one as a small child, pressing his eye to the lens and twisting the tin end to crate a variety of beautiful, perfectly symmetrical patterns. It seemed very small in his hands, very cold, very fragile.

He stood in the middle of the room. The windows were open, and he could hear the sound of birds and the water lapping and people talking outside. The air was heated and still, a perfect summer day. He didn't want to go home. He didn't know where home was. Perhaps it was here, inside this kaleidoscope toy. Perhaps it was elsewhere. All he had to do was look through the eye piece and twist the end. The urge was almost too much to bear, too much to resist.

Instead he crushed it in his hand before he weakened. It wasn't metal at all. The fibres seemed to crumble between his fingers, turn to dust and evaporate into the air. Trelawney felt a brief tug of loss, the last vestige of that lost part of his life, gone for good.

He packed his bags and he called for a taxi to take him to the train station.

~ 9 ~

There was a small piece on the BBC News website that caught Trelawney's eye several months later. He wouldn't have noticed it but for recognising the name.

Cumbria Police are appealing for information following a suspicious fire at Woodholme Manor, Castlerigg, just after midnight on Sunday. The manor house, owned by an Austrian hedge fund manager is the site of a private health clinic.

The blaze was brought under control by the Cumbria Fire and Rescue Service, and following a thorough search of the building, six people were recovered and taken to hospital

Trelawney made his way across Camden and walked through the market stalls to Camden Lock. He sat waiting in the sunshine with a sandwich he'd bought from Pret A Manger. The last glorious breath of the summer seemed to transform London into someplace else. Perhaps he was only seeing it with new eyes now he was leaving it all behind. He'd resigned his position at the bank that he couldn't recall being interviewed for. He'd handed over his keys to the house he shared with the professional couple in Putney. Today was the day that everything changed.

He thought of Costello sometimes and he wondered about his wife, wanting to forget him so much she was willing to erase him entirely from her memory. And what was left of that life? A woman in a care home with early onset dementia, being looked after by the man she'd paid Memoriae to forget. Trelawney wondered if

Costello was satisfied now. He wondered if all of the memories in his casual atrocity bag had finally degraded. He wondered if he believed what he had written: *Embrace the exquisite present! Before you know it, everything is beginning again.*

After a few minutes, Trelawney heard her footsteps on the towpath. He squinted up into the sun. She was smiling and the world was slowing down already, reordering itself around that smile. All of the light was rushing back in.

"Hello, Dennis," she said, and then they began.

Violent Men, Lonely Men

On my fifteenth birthday my father moved his mistress into the house. Cynthia was not much older than I was. Just out of those awkward years that I was still mired in: the constantly fluctuating friendships at the all-girls school I attended; deciding just what it was I wanted from the rest of my life, attempting to convince myself that it was more important than my father would have me believe. "Just get a job at Tesco, or something," he said, more than once. "Don't try to be someone you're not." My father should never have had a child. He would often regale guests and family with his notion that children were largely parasitical beings who burdened you for a good eighteen years and then you had grounds enough to turf them out so they could fend for themselves. His family was from Bolton, grindingly poor. He grew up in the shadow of the textile mills. His father had died when he was a child and his mother brought him and his four brothers up on a widow's pension. He despised the middle class, which was odd, because Mother was from much more genteel stock; her parents were civil servants and they'd raised their children in a pretty, rural hamlet in Hampshire. Mum and Dad had met at a dance when they were both teenagers; Mum with her beehive and her mini-skirt, Dad with his thick forearms, already sleeved in tattoos. Cheap rings on his fingers, perfect hair, winkle-pickers, just the right amount of self-confidence and charm. I've seen photos of them at that time. They seem like entirely different people to me now.

Mum stayed at the house for some time after Dad moved Cynthia in. For the first few days it wasn't as awkward as you might imagine. Cynthia was like a house-guest. The only real difference was evident in the evening. After Mum had slipped off to the spare bedroom at eight p.m., Cynthia shyly joined Dad on the sofa, pulling her slender legs up beneath her and nestling into his side while he watched the TV.

Later I would hear them retire to bed and have loud and mercifully brief sex. I think the fantasy of moving a younger woman into the marital home and my mother listening while he fucked her was probably a touch too stimulating for my father. It was mostly over before it began for Cynthia. She didn't seem dissatisfied or even particularly discomfited by the strange situation she'd found herself in. Indeed, within a couple of weeks my mother's deference about her marriage crumbling and her position being usurped only made it easier to accept this stranger into our home. Cynthia grew confident. She began to take over cooking family meals and preparing my school lunch. I couldn't find it in myself to dislike her particularly; she was only four years older than me, and, as I'd grown up without siblings, she quickly took on that role; an unlikely older sister figure and confidante. I could talk to her about boys, and my hopes for the future; away from here, from my parents shattered marriage and this place in the arse-hole end of the Black Country, where the streets and houses all looked the same.

But there was this: Our narrow house – 13 Birdsall Terrace, which sat at the end of a cul-desac packed with parked cars – was different to all of the others. The house had a dark history. Long before my parents had moved in a woman had been murdered here. She had been enticed back one night in the 60s by Matthew Priest, who was dubbed the 'Black Country Ripper' by the tabloid press. In 1976 he was convicted of murdering eleven women and attempting to murder eight others. He is serving twenty concurrent sentences of life imprisonment, which was increased to a whole life order in 2014. He began by assaulting the vulnerable young prostitutes who congregated a few roads away in our local red light district. His first murder victim was Irene Harrison, a young single mother. She was 23. Irene had escaped an abusive husband. She had discovered she was pregnant with his child and stole away quietly in the night, catching two buses and a train to sleep in her aunt's spare bedroom and start her life anew. She got a new job as a secretary in a solicitor's office in Birmingham City centre, had her baby and rented a flat a couple of miles away from Matthew Priest in Rye. It had been her first night out after the pregnancy; her aunt was looking after Lily, the beautiful young daughter that she doted on, even though she could see the abusive husband in her big grey eyes. Matthew Priest was a handsome man at the age of 33. You've doubtless seen photos of him, or watched the documentary film that was transmitted on BBC1 and then Netflix: tall; Paul Newman-blue eyes and sandy hair; impeccably dressed; a softly spoken manner. His reticence was what attracted Irene; I don't know that for a fact, of course; she's dead. She died four feet away from where my bed was as a child. But try as I might, I could not commune with spirits, and so her final actions on that night remain largely a mystery. But I can see the allure. Whether it was loneliness or simply lust that cajoled Irene Harrison away from that dance and into Matthew Priest's car, we'll probably never know. What we do know is that once she was at 13 Birdsall Terrace, and upstairs on the broad landing, Priest struck her twice with a hammer before stabbing her fifteen times in the neck, chest and abdomen. He reportedly panicked, stuffed her remains into three heavy-duty refuse sacks and then buried her in the narrow back garden.

He continued to live at Birdsall Terrace for another three years and, despite being interviewed five times in the course of their investigation, eluded the police for eight more. The manhunt was woefully mishandled, allowing him to slip through the net and kill a subsequent twelve women. He claimed that he heard the voice of God telling him to murder 'fallen' women in his head.

That old chestnut.

By the time he was arrested he'd changed address several times. The house where he'd killed Irene Harrison was home to two other families until my Mum and Dad moved in during the heatwave of 1976. I was fourteen. My parents' marriage was already floundering; my father's indiscretions growing more and more frequent. By the time we were settled, the temperatures were cresting 30°C, my father had moved Cynthia into our house, and Matthew Priest had finally been caught.

It didn't take long for the press to discover that he'd lived at 13 Birdsall Terrace. For a couple of days we had journalists knocking at our door or ringing our phone. Dad even discovered one of them rooting through our bins early one morning as he left for work. It wasn't too early for Dad to knock seven bells out of the young chancer. He was still lying bleeding in the road when I left for school – I had to step over him while he whimpered quietly in the foetal position.

I vividly recall the day we found out about Irene Harrison. It was nearing the end of summer and the temperature had dropped enough that you could sit outside comfortably in the afternoon. Dad had organised a barbecue. A handful of work mates, one of his brothers and his wife, a couple of the neighbours. Cynthia was firmly ensconced in the family home at that point; I remember sitting in their bedroom that afternoon before the guests arrived while she anxiously tried on various dresses. I lay on my side, flicking through a magazine, glancing up when she turned from the mirror to twirl for me.

"What do you think, Butterfly?" she asked, again and again. My name wasn't Butterfly. She just liked to call me that.

"You look perfect in *everything*," I would say petulantly. I was at that age where I'd convinced myself that nothing looked right on me. I was too tall, too awkward in my own skin, deeply aware of my acne and my stooped shoulders. In contrast, Cynthia was clearly the butterfly;

although with the benefit of half a century's hindsight, I realise that she was just a plain girl at best, buoyed up by my father's often exaggerated attentions and my mother's vastly diminished role in the household. Sometimes that's enough to make you fly.

"You'll realise soon," she said.

"Realise what?"

She cupped my chin and smiled. "How very beautiful you are, Butterfly." There was a delicate porcelain quality to her voice. Her parents came from Cambridge. Her father wrote scripts for sit-coms and her mother was an NHS administrator. God only knows what they thought about where their daughter had ended up. I think my father enjoyed the fact that he'd managed to break the resolve of two rather middle-class women with his dubious charms. Some of the flash and edge had gone out of his game by this time; middle-age spread was imminent and his hair was beginning to thin, which bothered him more than he'd admit. But he'd been bolstered by the thrill of the hunt with Cynthia, and further invigorated with his subsequent seduction and my mother's capitulation.

We found him presiding over some pathetic sausages and burgers out in the narrow back garden. He was wearing my mother's old apron and there were already five empty beer bottles beside the barbecue. A couple of work-mates and their wives were already there, as well as Dad's two younger brothers with their families in tow.

"Cyn!" he shouted as we stepped out of the back door. He flung an arm around Cynthia's shoulders and kissed her deeply on the lips. I looked away, feeling a deep and unexpected flush of shame. The guests simply gaped at him: clearly no one had been made aware of the change in our family's circumstances. "*This,*" my father exclaimed, beer sloshing out of his glass, "is Cynthia. Madam Cyn, I like to call her." He pushed Cynthia into the imagined limelight and patted her on the arse. I coloured further.

I kid you not, and I remember this perfectly: you could hear a fucking pin drop.

One of Dad's brothers was the first to ask the obvious question. "Where's Janet, Allan?"

Dad shrugged. He was already slightly pickled and his movements were ungainly. "Fuck knows," he said. "Probably in her room, sulking as usual."

To her credit, Cynthia tried to be hospitable, but this was clearly a step too far for suburbia in the seventies. Maybe some of them thought they'd be expected to drop their keys in an ashtray after they finished their hot dogs. Dad's guests nodded and smiled but generally gave her short shrift. A couple of hours later, Dad was well into his cups and only four or five guests remained, I think purely to observe how the situation would decline. They knew my Dad well. Sure enough a late-comer, one of Dad's old drinking buddies, stumbled in though the back gate and announced, "Fuck me, Allan, go on; where is she then?"

My dad, his wits slowed, assumed this was another opportunity to wheel Cynthia back out for our consideration. She and I were sitting on the rickety bench Dad had made at the bottom of the garden, picking at the last of the incinerated burgers.

Dad's mate stumbled into the centre of the garden and jabbed at the dry earth with the toe of his shoes. "We gonna dig her up or what?"

There was a moment of dawning horror on the remainder of the guests' faces, concluding that, because they still hadn't seen hide nor hair of my mother, my dad had indeed done away with her and buried her in the back garden.

"*The fuck* you talking about, Eric?" My dad, having relinquished the culinary complexities of the barbecue, was at a loss, and subsequently quick to temper. As a household we were all too aware of that aspect of his nature. His shortcomings were, as I'm sure you're coming to grasp, multifarious.

"The Ripper!" Eric cried. "You know, the fucking Ripper."

"What about him, you daft bastard?"

"His first victim. It was *here*. Right bastard *here*. He's said as much to the police. Haven't you seen it on the news?"

Dad only watched the news for football results.

"He killed her in the house and buried her in the back garden," Eric said. "*This* fucking back garden."

Again. Fucking pin drop silence.

A couple of old police detectives arrived not long after the last guests had left. Dad had staggered into the corner of the garden to piss in a plant pot and then went to sleep off the afternoon's excesses. Cynthia answered the door and was happy to defer all responsibility to my mother, who came downstairs, demure and every inch the adult that Cynthia couldn't possibly hope to be for at least another ten years or so. Mum had removed herself gradually from the running of the house in light of being relegated to the back bedroom. She and my father had fought initially, but she had, of late, simply absolved herself of all responsibility and become, to all intents and purposes, a lodger. It was like having another teenager in the house; she got up late, she ate at odd hours and she would leave wet towels and laundry on the bathroom floor, just for the simple pleasure of knowing Cynthia would have to be the one who picked up after her.

But she sat down that evening with the detectives and, for a brief while, was returned to being the mother I knew from childhood. She told me to go to my room, but I loitered in the hallway with Cynthia, her finger to her lips to ensure I remained silent. Little acts like that only consolidated my affection for her.

The police were there to apprise my mother of the situation, and that they would, of course, be sending a forensics team in to excavate our garden in the next few days. They had no reason to be sceptical about this new nugget of information from Matthew Priest. Apparently God had insisted he reveal the identities of the other women he'd murdered, the ones they had never found, but suspected were his victims. My mother said, "Of course" a lot and insisted that they would assist the police however they could. I realise in retrospect that it was an opportunity for her to shake things up; perhaps she sensed that there was only one natural conclusion to this state of affairs, so the exhumation of a body was simply another avenue to travel down before admitting defeat to my father and packing her bags.

Rather predictably, Dad hit the roof when he realised that my mother had invited the local constabulary to park outside his house and pitch up their white tents in his back garden. It was neither here nor there; the police weren't asking his permission.

I didn't have a lot of friends, and school was a fucking nightmare. Rumours about my family situation had spread like a forest fire, which went some way to ostracising me. I had no idea how to articulate how I felt about the situation, so I didn't. The girls thought I was odd, cold, aloof. They were right. I am all of those things, more so because of those awkward fraught years. It took me a long time to distance myself from those things, to meet the right man, to learn I was neither of my parents and not doomed to repeat their mistakes. I repeatedly attempted just that during my twenties, testing man after man with my behaviour. None of them deserved the woman I was then.

I was, I freely admit, a bit of shit.

So instead of friends, my only real confidante was my father's mistress, which was its own psychological minefield and a future bonanza for my assorted psychiatrists. Cynthia and I would lie in my bed together sometimes, when she tired of my father's sexual overtures. The initial fire of their ardour had dimmed somewhat at this point, and I think he was glad for some peace alone in his own bed, away from a small terrace house filled with three women who were all wise to his bullshit. But when Cynthia was otherwise occupied I became fixated with Matthew Priest's reign of terror.

I watched the forensics officers working into the night that first day, the lights on in their tent, people in white overalls coming and going, detectives smoking in our yard. They weren't like the kind you saw on TV. They were usually quite underwhelming specimens: overweight, balding, unshaven, often quite coarse, even during such a fraught investigation.

I watched all of the TV reports on the case, quietly collated newspaper clippings from *The Sun* when my dad folded them up and put them in the bin. I imagined Matthew Priest inhabiting this narrow house, moving around it, sleeping in the main bedroom, sitting watching TV downstairs; all of the routine aspects of a life. But then there were the more shrouded facets to his character which took me some time to divine; to properly grasp how someone could decide to go out one night, pretend to be just some ordinary young man with the same desires and impulses as any other, and then bring a woman back to their house and murder them. I read the articles about Irene Harrison, the young single mother whom Priest had elected to pick up that night and bring home to murder. The very notion that this woman had already endured domestic abuse before having no other recourse but to steal away in the night and start her life again was a wretched state of affairs to begin with. That she had done just that, embarked on a new career, rented a flat, and given birth to the child of her abusive spouse, only compounded the abject, arbitrary cruelty of life to me. She didn't *deserve* the cards she had been dealt. She had begun again. She had probably thought long and hard about 'getting back out there' as they put it; getting dressed up, feeling those familiar butterflies about a night out, and all of the inherent possibilities. And then she had met the handsome stranger with Paul Newman-blue eyes, and allowed herself to be attracted enough by his apparently tender nature that she would take a chance on a night with him. How much fortitude must it have taken to trust another man after what she'd endured with her ex-husband? But then he'd taken her upstairs, produced a hammer, struck her twice in the face and stabbed her repeatedly until she was dead. At fifteen I didn't know what I believed about a higher power – my parents had no particular religious leanings – but I do recall thinking what an awful waste it was and how very cruel. It made me feel melancholy in ways I'd never felt before; it made me realise that we were essentially alone in the world. That Irene Harrison's fate should not have been so unnecessarily severe was, I supposed, nothing more than a moralistic fallacy.

I would stand on the narrow landing, with the bare wooden staircase behind me, and cast around for some psychic residue of the event. Surely, I thought, such a violent act must leave an imprint in the air and the walls and floorboards of this house. That it somehow echoed backwards and forwards through time for other generations to hear, drowning out all of the usual sounds of normal domesticity. I would get down on my hands and knees and study the bare floorboards, the skirting board, looking for the merest shadow of a stain of Irene Harrison's blood. I listened for the stone tape of trauma, perhaps somehow absorbed and recorded into the walls and floors of 13 Birdsall Terrace. I thought that if I lay in my bed at night with the door open and stared hard into the gloom I might glimpse some fragment of the event, recurring endlessly. All it required was some tuned-in soul such as me as witness. Instead only an oppressive silence remained; on empty Saturday afternoons it seemed to surge up out of the rooms towards me. Maybe I just wanted Irene not to feel alone when she died, that she could look forwards and see me tucked inside my bed with my eyes wide and she would feel less abandoned by the absent morals of the world.

Perhaps I was just a morbid little shit. It was probably that.

In any event the police dug up most of the garden and found nothing to suggest that any remains existed there. Irene was not where Matthew Priest had insisted he'd laid the pieces of her to rest. Perhaps the forest fire in his brain that night had occluded the order of events for him and he was mistaken. My father had watched from the kitchen window as they moved their search from one place to another, beer in his hand, everything else forgotten. All he would say at the end of it was: "All that effort for nothing. She's not even there. And now my rockery is properly fucked."

My mother finally moved out not long after that. She'd found a nice flat in a large, dusty Victorian house in Walsall, near the Arboretum. It happened quite quickly. One day she sat me down and told me she had packed her bags while Dad was at work, and that a friend was coming to collect them. The friend was a man she'd met called Neal. The cases were all lined up in the hall when he arrived. It was so sudden, I didn't know how to feel. But once Neal had loaded the last of the cases into the back of his Cortina estate and Mum came back in to kiss me goodbye, I felt a flood of abandonment and fear at being left alone with my dad as the sole parent. His relationship with Cynthia was already showing signs of wear. With increased confidence she'd enrolled in evening classes at the local college to study hairdressing, and become a junior at a salon down the road. Suddenly she was experimenting on my own dowdy long hair with a blow dryer and a large bristle brush. My dad called it the 'tug and burn dry'. But she'd gradually begun to improve, and she was making new friends. My dad didn't really like that; a wider circle would only impress upon her the mistakes she'd made by shacking up with him. The idea that one day Cynthia would come to her senses and also leave made me anxious about being here alone with my father. I wasn't exactly scared of him, I simply didn't *like* him.

After a few weeks, once Mum was settled, I started going over to her flat on the weekend. Neal would arrive and beep his horn. The first time he came over he made the mistake of coming to the door. My dad was expecting him and he was already thoroughly shit-faced. He started shouting and pushing Neal backwards until they were both wrestling without much conviction in the tiny square of front garden. I stood in the doorway with my holdall filled with a change of clothes and some toiletries for the weekend. They rolled around for a couple of interminable minutes, both of them covered in grass and cat shit until my dad was half-unconscious. Neal got up, picked up his broken glasses, dusted himself off and looked at me. "Shall we?" he said, mustering a pained smile. I stepped over my father, who was already snoring loudly, Neal rolled him onto his side and we left him there with the neighbours' kids all staring at him from the garden wall.

Neal generally left me and mum alone for the first few visits. I vividly remember those weekends; although my mum didn't have much – a living room and kitchenette, a bathroom and bedroom, all of them with tall ceilings with her meagre possessions scattered around them – she did have the Walsall Arboretum on her doorstep. It's always summer in these memories

I have, half a lifetime away, and we are walking, me, my mum and her new dog, Milo – a noisy little Yorkshire terrier who was convinced he was a Doberman – around that lovely Victorian park. The lake, the bandstand, the pavilion, the long walks that would always end with an ice cream for me; I can still lose myself in those memories. I was almost 16 at that point, but I discovered with Mum gone that I had obviously taken her parenting for granted; I missed her terribly. Now that Cynthia was spending more time at the hairdressing salon during the day and at the college a couple of evenings a week, the house was suddenly very quiet. My dad had disappeared inside himself; with Mum gone, Cynthia growing into her new horizons, and me on the cusp of flying the nest, he must have realised that life, the life he'd had, the fantasy life he'd made, and whatever it was he really craved, was slowly but surely slipping through his fingers. Sometimes Mum would ask how things were going between Dad and Cynthia, but not very often; I don't think she really cared when all was said and done. She harboured no residual feelings of affection for my father; after what he'd done I expect it would have been easy to hate him; she didn't, she simply pitied him. I told her about Cynthia's new job and college course without a thought. After a moment, she smiled. "Good for her," she said.

Dad rebuilt his rockery, laid down new turf. Sometimes I would come downstairs of an evening and find him sitting in the dark, staring out of the window at the garden as if trying to divine where Matthew Priest had buried Irene Harrison. The murder itself didn't seem to occupy him as much as the insistence from Priest that he had buried Irene in our garden. But the police had been thorough. Irene wasn't there. It started to consume him. He found my scrapbook of news clippings one day, but he hadn't lost his temper. He'd simply claimed it for himself, poring over my paltry attempts at collating the story of Matthew Priest.

By this point, he was barely speaking to me. Soon I would start college, make friends, find a boy who doted on me and lose my virginity; I'd move out and live in a grubby bedsit with a promiscuous girl called Mandy. My father had abandoned me already. I was simply a stranger who lived upstairs in his narrow house.

One evening I came home to find him

digging in the back garden. Judging by the depth of the hole he'd been at the back breaking labour for the better part of an afternoon. "What are you doing, Dad?" I asked.

He glanced up at me, momentarily bewildered. "Pond," he said. As if in confirmation he glanced around at the hole he was standing in. "Yes. A fish pond. I've always wanted Koi."

When I woke up the next day, I discovered that he had filled the hole in and dug another while I slept. He'd been out there all night, eventually down to his vest and underpants. I stood beside Cynthia at the window. "He's off his trolley," she said, lighting a cigarette. She'd only just taken up smoking and she did it with panache, as if she were a character from a French movie; at the time it seemed to give her a thrillingly cosmopolitan edge; I took up smoking as soon as I could once I moved out. It took me thirty years to quit, so I have Cynthia to blame for *that*.

"He told me he was putting a pond in," I said.

"He's looking for her."

"But the police looked."

"I know. He told me he has dreams about her."

"Irene? Why?"

Cynthia released a perfect plume of smoke and glanced at me. "Search me, Butterfly. He's been like this ever since the police left. Like I said, he's going potty in his old age."

"Should I tell Mum?"

She shook her head and her hair moved like a slow wave. Her hair really was brilliant since she'd started working at the hair salon. "She knows. I told her the other day."

"*You* talk to Mum?"

She smiled. "Your mum's brilliant. I sometimes do her hair."

This was information that I was ill-prepared for. I had drawn up mental demarcation lines between my fractured family and had decided without much contemplation that my mum and Cynthia were on opposing sides. I hadn't lived enough life at that point to expect the unexpected of people. They really are fucking weird sometimes. With a parting glance at my father, looking like an expectant archaeologist searching for bone fragments in his underwear, we left for our respective days.

A week later the relationship between Cynthia and my father came to an abrupt but certain end. It was a Sunday. They had been bickering on and off all weekend while I tried to remain in my room, listening to records and reading books. The garden was in ruins. It looked like a bomb had been detonated out there, and all that remained were mounds of uprooted turf and deep trenches in the ground. The neighbours' cat had gotten stuck down one of them and started crying in the middle of the night. One of the kids had to be lowered down with a tin of Whiskas to coerce the thing back out again. Dad was slowly going around the bend; we were all on the same page with that, but lately he'd been snapping at Cynthia, insulting her about her weight, her hair, her intelligence; a gradual war of nerves that Cynthia had no interest in competing in, although Dad was the easiest of targets by this time. He'd fallen into middle age without an ounce of grace; he was half-cut most days, he'd outgrown all of his shirts due to an ever-expanding beer belly, his hair was almost gone save for a few wisps that he struggled valiantly with each morning and his friends had all but left him behind. When he went to the pub on the corner, he largely sat alone, nursing one

Guinness after another until chucking out time. Once he'd been the alpha-male of his particular circle of friends, now they cut him a wide berth; they'd tired of his diatribes and the danger of his open racism, his constant talk of Matthew Priest. Dad spoke about him as if they were old friends; he thought there was some strange caché involved in living in a prodigious murderer's former house. My dad had once sat at the top of a crane every day, looking down on the city below him; now he'd been laid off, forced into drawing the dole; I think he secretly despised himself for how far he'd fallen when he'd started so low. Instead, the brunt of his anger was shouldered by Cynthia. I realise now that she only remained to safeguard me from his ire. But everyone has their limit and that Sunday we reached Cynthia's.

"At least I'm working!" she shouted across the dining table. We still upheld the absurd ritual of eating at the table, even with Mum gone. Cynthia had taken on the role of cooking for us without a word of complaint. Every evening, even the ones when she was attending her evening classes, there was food on the table for all of us. I realise now that she was a fucking saint.

"As a bleeding *junior* at a hairdressers!"

"Better that than looking for some poor girl's remains and getting pissed every day!"

"I don't have to listen to this!"

"That's your problem, you've never *listened* to anyone your entire fucking miserable life!"

My father stood up so violently that his chair fell backwards. He swept his plate off the table, took hold of Cynthia's hair and yanked her towards him. Then he slapped her with the full force of the back of his hand. It all happened in seconds. Before I could stand, Cynthia was sprawled across the carpet, her cheek bright red, her left eye closed.

For a moment, everything was silent and charged with the sudden eruption of violence. My dad looked down at her, his face filled with conflicting emotions. No, not emotions. I'm not sure he was entirely capable of those; men of his generation and upbringing were stiff and unyielding, unable to show joy or remorse unless they were at a football match. Perhaps it was shame. But whatever it was he felt, it soon passed and he turned away from us, went and sat out in the remains of the garden with a beer and a packet of Embassy Regal.

Cynthia was packed and ready to leave by 9 p.m. that evening. I could see that she'd struggled with the absolute need to leave and remaining simply to shield me from harm. But I understood, even though it made me afraid to be the one left behind. I *understood*. I couldn't really believe that she'd stayed this long.

"Where will you go?" I asked.

"I have friends," she said with a sad smile. She touched my face. "There's always someone."

"Will you keep in touch?" I asked.

"Butterfly, of *course* I will. We'll meet up and go out. Once you're old enough you'll be out of here too. You can come and live with me. As soon as I'm settled I'll call you and give you my phone number."

I didn't hear Dad come inside that night. It must have been long after I'd gone to bed and fallen asleep. I'd expected him to erupt as soon as he discovered Cynthia had left, and for him to burst into my room demanding to know where she'd gone. But in the days that followed the subject was never raised once. Indeed, he barely spoke to me. I did sense that something had gone out of him in those subsequent weeks. I don't think any amount of preparation for being abandoned would have been sufficient. He drank more, smoked more, sat outside and stared emptily at the garden, lost inside his own self-pity. I would make dinner for us both and tell him to come inside; when he didn't I took the plate out into the garden for him. He never ate any of it.

Not long after my mum moved in with Neal, I think ostensibly so that there would be room for me to live with them, which I did gladly. The day they came round to move my things, Dad was out. We made light work of my room, Neal and I, while my mum wandered around the house, tutting to herself at the layer of dust on surfaces and the general malaise in every room.

"Look at the garden!" she said to Neal once we'd loaded up his car. "It's an absolute disgrace."

She eventually got a divorce and married Neal. He was a kind, uncomplicated man, a low-paid civil servant who mended broken watches in the evening. He was nothing at all like my father. I don't wish to imply that he was any less interesting than my father because he was staid and wholly even tempered. There wasn't an angry bone in his body. I thought he was lovely, precisely because he was simply a good man. My mother valued him all the more for having come out the other side of a shitty marriage. I'd thought that this was the second chance Irene Harrison hadn't been afforded, but then Mum died three years later of breast cancer and I realised that there is hurt in the notion of fair. We want to impose a sense of justice on an unjust world. All of our beliefs reassure us that there is fairness in life that isn't always visible. I dwelled on this for some time after she died. I was at university by this time, so I had already moved out. When I returned, it wasn't really my home anymore, although Neal insisted that I stay as long as I wanted. Not long after I met a young man called Jonathan. He'd had polio as a child and it had left him with a slight limp. He was kind and reminded me more of Neal than my dad; I think I spent a good portion of my twenties and thirties measuring men by that yardstick. It lasted a year, it ended because of me; the psychological warfare of my childhood was beginning to emerge in long paralysing bouts of depression and anxiety that continue to this day.

Almost thirty years after Irene Harrison's

murder, she was finally discovered. A television production company contacted my father in 1997. They were intending to make a new documentary about the Black Country Ripper and his victims. They had discovered that, two years after Matthew Priest had sold 13 Birdsall Terrace, the council had issued a Compulsory Purchase Order for twelve square feet of land at the foot of each of the back gardens on Birdsall Terrace to 'facilitate the carrying out of development, re-development or improvement'. In plain terms the boundary line of each of the back gardens was shortened. The documentary makers had already looked into Land Registry deeds and uncovered the initial paperwork for the CPO, issued in 1973. This suggested that when Matthew Priest had insisted that he had buried Irene Harrison in his back garden, he had not necessarily been lying, even though the police had not uncovered evidence in our garden.

My dad had continued to live in the house long after we'd all moved on. In his later years he cut a much reduced figure; he had long been unemployed due to almost crippling arthritis. At some point he'd stopped drinking and smoking after the GP warned him that if he continued he'd almost certainly see an early grave. It gave him some much needed clarity. After getting my degree I had moved to Gloucester to work for an assessment team in social service, and by the 90s I had returned to the Midlands to work as a senior social worker for a child protection team in Wolverhampton. I would drop in to see my father as often as I could manage. By now he was an easier man to spend time with; sober, reflective, often quite astute about his situation and the past. He was all-too aware of the mistakes he'd made. He sometimes contested that the financial and emotional poverty of his upbringing had been a factor in his poor conduct towards my mother and Cynthia. I stopped short of telling him there had always been a choice; if he had considered himself and his behaviour earlier, he might have been a kinder man who'd made better decisions. He read voraciously; there were dog-eared paperback thrillers and a smattering of Penguin Modern Classics piled up beside his armchair. He made little models out of bits of cardboard too. They were quite poor; Dad had very little artistic ability but he displayed them around the house with pride. Seeing them made me feel melancholy for some reason; when he told me over the phone that he was making these little constructions I'd hoped they might be better than they were, that these models would perhaps represent him and his experience, but they looked like children's compositions. They made him happy: I suppose that means something.

He'd never really let the business of Matthew Priest and Irene Harrison go in all those years. He still had the little scrapbook of newspaper articles that I'd put together when I was fifteen, still leafed though it from time to time, mentioned it in passing when I'd come by. Despite the arthritis he'd remodelled the garden, only paying for help when his plans exceeded his abilities. It was pretty now. It had a decked area and a pond, some raised beds and a magnolia tree as its centrepiece. When I'd visit during the summer months we'd sit outside and eat lunch and watch the birds and squirrels nibble at the feeders he'd put out. We'd talk about my job and he'd talk about the neighbours or one of the books he'd read. His world was much reduced. He had no friends to speak of anymore, so my visits were a lifeline to him. I found it difficult to hold onto any past malice I harboured for the way he'd treated my mother and Cynthia. He said he saw Cynthia from time to time. She now owned the hair salon where she'd apprenticed at all those years ago; she was married to an ex-Aston Villa footballer who drove a classic E-type Jaguar. Every now and then they'd pass on the high street and she'd glance at him without really acknowledging him.

"I should talk to her one of these days," he'd say, sadly. "But I suppose it's been too long now. What do you think?"

"I'd leave it alone, Dad," I'd say. "Water under the bridge and all that."

Cynthia and I had kept in touch for several years after she left my dad, although we never quite achieved the level of closeness that she'd promised. We went out on the town a few times while I was in college and I slept on her floor after parties. But with the family connection between us severed that sisterly relationship gradually fizzled out. She had three kids with the footballer and they'd lived in a beautiful house near Kenilworth until he lost a good portion of his investments due to gambling debts. They lived well enough and the hair salon kept them afloat, even though they had to move to a two bedroom semi in Stourbridge. I hadn't seen her in years.

"What's this about the TV crew then Dad?" I asked. "Are they coming to interview you?"

Dad explained the claim about boundary lines and the CPO from the council.

"So our garden used to be longer?"

"A good twelve feet longer," dad said. "The council bought it intending to develop the land, build new houses, but nothing ever happened, even after they'd changed the boundary lines. This was all well before we moved in."

"So they're suggesting that Matthew Priest wasn't lying. That maybe he did bury Irene Harrison here, just in that twelve feet of garden that used to belong to him."

"It never did feel right to me," my dad said, "that he would lie about something like that. What's the point?"

"He thought God was telling him to kill women Dad. He was a nutter."

My dad smiled. "Yes, granted, there was that."

"Still, you'd have thought the police would have discovered that at the time, wouldn't you?"

"You're fucking joking, aren't you? Did you see them? Fat bastards, loafing around, smoking and joking and wolf-whistling women. They couldn't organise a gang-bang in a nunnery."

"Dad. Really?"

"Well anyway, they're making this documentary and they're coming around to film up on the landing and in the back garden. Think they're going to interview me too. Paying me for the luxury, mind."

"Are they going to excavate the land that the council bought?"

"Oh yes," my dad said. "I suppose they're hoping it'll be the centrepiece of the documentary. Assuming Irene is down there, waiting for them."

He stared out hopefully at the garden and the land beyond. I couldn't tell what it was that he felt had passed him by in that regard. Irene Harrison had never really meant anything to us, never belonged to us in any real way. But she had died here in this narrow house, turned it into a box full of darkness. She'd haunted us a little bit. Maybe the tragedy of the event had imbued us all with some sadness that we'd carried inside us. I'm not sure. It sounds far too melodramatic for my liking. But I put my hand on his and said: "Go and get a nice haircut before they come, eh? Look nice for the cameras."

He did. He put on his best shirt and pullover and he was freshly shaved that day. They filmed his little cardboard constructions and edited them in around the interview, which made me feel a deep well of sorrow for him, but he was quite proud that they were featured. They did dig up that crucial twelve square feet beyond our garden and there she was in the final episode of the show, the sad skeletal remains of Irene Harrison, buried four feet down, separated into three bin bags which had disintegrated years ago. It was a full stop to the mystery of Irene's death. I actually felt as if some invisible weight had lifted from me, from my family on that day, although none of us would have been able to quantify that weight. I watched the footage of the remains of the bones. It seemed like a paltry representation of a life; 23 years old, murdered and buried and almost forgotten. Although that's not true at all. I'd not forgotten her in all those years, and neither had Dad.

"I always think about houses," my dad said when they interviewed him. "And what we fill them with. Kids and parties and kissing and sleeping and eating. But they're still just bricks and mortar and joists and pipes. They don't have memories."

Dad died a couple of years later. He went downhill after they found Irene. I think that was all he'd been waiting for. A full-stop on something that had lingered around him every day of his life in this house, no matter whether he believed it had memories or not. After he was gone, I went about emptying the house alone. I was newly divorced and my life felt like a raw nerve. Every item of clothing, every silly cardboard model found fresh tears in me. But I bagged everything up and emptied the place, holding onto a few keepsakes for myself. The house sold quickly to a young family. I heard that they'd ripped everything out and started again. I don't know if they ever found out that 13 Birdsall Terrace was a 'murder house'. Eventually it would be forgotten entirely; a secret history, a sadness that had gone away the day they found Irene's bones.

I remarried and had three kids. Beautiful

things, they were, with their father's blue eyes and good nature. We upped sticks and bought a house in St Ives in Cornwall. Five minutes walk away from the sea. I retired from social work and then the kids flew the nest to lives of their own. My husband died last year from pneumonia complications. Now I tend a pretty little garden with a magnolia tree of my own and all of these things I have told you feel very far away and yet very much a part of who I am today. I've realised that what defines you more than anything else is your ability to move on even when you've lost perspective. Happiness can be a memorial for all the losses in your life.

Today Matthew Priest died. He was 84. It was on the news. There was a brief photo of him at the age of 33 with his Paul Newman-blue eyes. They didn't mention Irene, of course. She was just one of his victims, a long-forgotten woman. But I'll remember her. I'll be happy for her.

~ 1 ~

1975. By ten p.m. Daniel had peaked. His producer sent him home to Haverstock Hill in a taxi. Clutching his guitar case between those spindly legs of his, Danny saw London through a dope haze. He'd scored some powerful skunk-weed called Black Pearl from a hippy commune in Wiltshire some months ago, before his problems began. He was catching glimpses of what he was becoming, he wrote in that first letter; and, like a diminishing point on the horizon, what he used to be.

That night he'd dreamt he was tethered to a string, like a roaming kite. The sky pulled him up into itself and he had no choice but to acquiesce.

"There aren't any choices anymore," he wrote. "I go where the river flows."

The day was dawning; a brittle light was falling through London's cracks and hollows – Danny saw it all with a rare, piercing insight. People were leaving their homes, making their way to unspecified jobs; trains had started to rattle towards destinations, feeding bodies like blood into and out of the heart of the city. He flew unseen above it all – the streets still cool before the sunlight had burnt through the haze – and woke on the Underground in his shirt and cords, barefoot, hair uncombed, heading south on the Northern Line, just leaving Camden Town. It was quiet by this time on the train: the mid-morning lull of housewives and slightly bewildered tourists and pensioners, exchanging hospital woes. Danny stood for a while, trying to determine where to alight, then seated himself again, confused, finally a little bit scared. It wasn't the first time that he'd woken to find himself beneath London; he believed that his body was luring him towards something his mind couldn't yet admit to.

He considered transferring and paying a visit to Sarah at her flat in Battersea, but thought better of it. His sister's face in his mind made him feel as if there was a hard stone in his chest, crushing his emotions. He had no idea how long he stayed on the train. It felt quiet inside him, he wrote, like being left alone inside a church. When he did finally propel himself up and out onto the platform, he was at Leicester Square.

There were some Americans clustered around the Underground map nearby. The volume of their voices made his mind feel barren; the way he felt after taking the medication his doctor had prescribed. They stared at his bare feet, and one of the younger ones laughed behind her hand. Daniel felt a spark of naked embarrassment and stumbled out to the escalators, mouthing the words on the frayed bill-posters like a mantra that might set him free from himself.

The brilliant light of a summer's day in Leicester Square paralysed him. People were chasing their shadows down the street, eyeing him with curious sideways glances. The traffic was a suffocating standstill; a radio was drifting music down from an open office window, playing something unfamiliar that he imagined Sarah or I might know.

The glimpse of someone nearby making gestures with his empty hands, as if he was folding air into boxes or origami shapes, made Danny doubly nervous. Perhaps he was a street magician, Danny mused, or a mime. But he swore he could hear his name being repeated out of gritted teeth, through the street noise: "DannyDannyDannyDanny…"

He felt a terrible sense of apprehension as he retraced his steps and pushed his way back down the escalator, reciting the poster mantra in reverse. It hadn't served him well forwards, and his seemed like a paltry ritual compared to the magician's at the station entrance. When he reached the platform, he could feel his shirt clinging to the small of his back, and the inside of his skull felt itchy with expectation. The heat and the noise of the sticky dinner-hour throng made him stumble closer to the edge of the platform. He could see tiny mice scurrying beneath the rails.

There was a rush of stale, summery air, and then Daniel stumbled clumsily out onto the tracks. Out of the corner of his narrowed vision he saw a huge dark shape, and faces behind him with mouths that had become dark Os. He felt no regret, he wrote, no sense of loss. In the slow soporific lull before the blackness and the terrible pain, Danny imagined that the train might stop in time, and cheat him.

~ 2 ~

Sarah's actions and words seemed slower now, more deliberate. She spoke in clipped, contemplated sentences. But it was nothing more or less than age. It had been almost fifty years. Even prize-fighters became more measured and circumspect in the later rounds. Had I changed too? I still felt clumsy beside her, a bit reckless; befuddled again by the clamour of my feelings. I discovered what I was saying when I said it. I always had.

When our emotions finally got in the way of what we were saying, our hands took over quite involuntarily, and we found ourselves at the end of an initially civilised evening on the edge of my bed, flustered and coy, refastening buttons and turning the lights back on.

"We don't have to do anything, sweet."

"No, I know that."

"There's plenty of time for that. All the time in the world."

"Yes. Yes of course."

After that we went downstairs, lit some candles that I found beneath the sink, opened some wine, and talked into the night. Sarah was still very proper and polite; quite upper-middle class, but coming to nursing in her mid-thirties had worn much of the reserve right out of her. She'd ended up in Birmingham during the eighties, a little bit lost after a divorce that had felt too clean and too easy a break from so many years of supposed love. "Too much equanimity," she said. "I felt obliged to be civilised. He remarried a couple of months later, of course. He'd been seeing this woman for two years while we were still married. Although she really wasn't a woman. She was nineteen. *Nineteen*. Bloody fool."

She ended up working in paediatrics before she retired, and I could imagine her as the lines gradually deepened in her face, strands of grey creeping through her curls; walking down some pale corridor, speaking softly to sick youngsters, sat unblinking in front of the telly, wrapped up in dressing-gowns, wearing silly slippers. "Just sit up, love, while we take your temperature."

As Sarah spoke in my living-room, I saw her falling asleep on her bus home, carrying a basket around Sainsbury's (she never needed a trolley), talking to her cat as it curled around her ankle when she opened the door to her flat in Stirchley, the radio on for noise, keys in the ashtray, a warm bath, drawing the curtains, reading in bed until she dozed off with a finger marking her place... It was romantic alchemy. We held hands as our shadows grew around the room, the wine making us drowsy. Her eyes kept glancing to the window, as if she was expecting someone; it kept jarring me awake. I wanted to ask why she'd really come back. I thought I could hear dogs scrapping outside, but when I looked there were only street-lamps, stooping in from the corner of the street, and after a while I was too exhausted to care. Sarah eventually closed the curtains and we went to bed.

In the morning I stood outside in the back yard in last night's clothes, watching my coffee go cold. Something had already changed in me. I could feel a warmth beneath my skin that had nothing to do with the July morning, unveiling itself as neighbours opened curtains, let dogs out to piss, turned on their radios. It was like vertigo.

Sarah came out with her coat over her arm. For a moment I glimpsed the girl from 1975, hiding between the lines of Danny's second letter. It had been waiting on the doormat in a plain envelope when I brought the milk in. I kept catching glimpses of us all then, when Sarah was not the only one to have hair past her shoulders; our history, like a shorthand of the years.

But my mind couldn't be trusted. I'd made Sarah extraordinary in her absence, given her more life than I could bear, too many happy years; I'd used too many colours, and instead here we were, waiting for the rug to be pulled from beneath us, still moving in the same diminished circles at seventy; lost and found, lost and found.

She kissed me and left her new phone number, written on my palm, like we were still teenagers, and left through the back gate.

~ 3 ~

Daniel returned to the Underground almost every day, as if he were courting a lover, or mourning a departed one. It was 1976 by this time, but the train continued to lead him out of sleep every morning, tons of steel emerging from the tunnel, and beyond that the same tableaux of memories in different arrangements.

Waking up in intensive care, having defied the odds and fallen beneath the tracks just seconds before the train arrived. Nonetheless, there was a clipboard at the end of his bed listing a league table of injuries. Days of morphine. A mélange of faces: Sarah, myself, his producer and sound engineer, someone from the record company, various musicians from Hampstead Heath, where most of us had digs back then. After a week or so he finally discovered that his left arm was gone below the elbow. Sarah tried to hold him but he wanted none of it; she talked to him as much as was possible, cut his hair, mothered him a bit. She was just relieved he was alive. Months of physiotherapy; feeling the pull of gravity after all that time on his back due to an additional spinal injury. Days of silence, which led Sarah to me, for someone to talk to. Eventually they transferred Danny to a psychiatric ward, where every face that stared back at him seemed impenetrable with medication. No progress, only pills. Danny had been here once before. He recognised the girl with the sickly smile who sat in the waiting room all day, pissing herself rather than move. Interminable hours spent staring out of the wire-reinforced windows of the day room, which smelled of cigarettes and stale farts, thinking about his guitar and the stump of his left arm; it felt like a joke waiting for a punch line. A couple of music journalists turned up looking for a story, but he wilfully baffled them with esoterica about black American blues guitarists from the forties and fifties. He had nothing to say to them.

By the turn of the year, Danny had slipped through the net. He still had his flat in a large, somewhat decrepit Victorian townhouse near Chalk Farm tube station, where an executive from his record company had his weekly stipend of £15 posted, despite the fact that there would clearly be no more recordings from Danny. He still had friends in high places who were deeply concerned for his welfare.

But he was rarely at the house. By this time he was fixated on the Underground. "I don't know why exactly," he wrote at that point, "but I daresay I shall find out. I just feel drawn."

In that second letter there were moments of startling clarity, then childish aimlessness. I remember him at that time: if he had once been a book of poetry, then he was steadily dwindling to verse, a word, a blank page. I envisioned him outside Victoria Station, hunched in the rain, with his jacket collar pulled up beneath his ears, staring at faces, looking for something: eyes as vacant or haunted as his own, perhaps; or the elusive street magician, folding air with his hands.

Daniel took shelter eventually. He hadn't realised how loud the rain sounded, he wrote, until he was in the cavernous shelter of the station. He caught voices, threads of conversations, like stray radio bands. A young lad was slumped in front of a coat, playing *Sad Eyed Lady of the Lowlands*. But it was background noise. There was another reason Danny was here:

"She was reading *Catch-22*..." he wrote, and my heart ached for him. Danny had been circling her all through spring, working up the nerve to make his approach. He'd bought the book himself, and couldn't quite fathom why. It was all alien territory to him. He was a love-struck adolescent. Finally he went over, fumbled some loose change from his long unwashed cords, and bought a bunch of tulips from her as the sound of station announcements sang in his ears like birdsong. He didn't say anything initially, of course; chronic shyness would take his voice from him at crucial moments such as these. But he had made the vital first approach.

"She was probably no more than twenty," he wrote. "She had very pale skin. She kept tugging the hem of her skirt down over her thighs, and then looking around nervously."

She too was waiting for someone to coax her out of her chrysalis. She said to him: "Are you Daniel Faulkner?"

"Yes," he mumbled, his eyes on his scuffed shoes. "I used to be, anyway."

"I have your record, you know. It's really very good."

Danny confused her by smiling, nodding mutely, then folding the stump of his arm in to his coat.

"Oh," she said, as if she'd only just grasped the connotation of his missing hand. He was suddenly painfully aware not only of that, but of his unwashed clothes and hair. He couldn't control his gaze; it was all he could do to ignore the nervous movement of her slender hands, the hair she pulled behind her ears. Every detail seemed vitally important to him. But Danny was at a loss. If these words were lines in a song, the situation would have been fine.

The girl hesitated, possibly baffled by his reticence, and went back to the stall to serve someone else. Danny walked away, deeper into the station. The girl observed him from behind Catch-22, bemused, no longer reading. Danny felt as if everyone in the station was watching, could read his sad, cloying mind. The busker was playing *Glass Onion*. The heat inside him made his shirt cling to his back. He smelt of rain and sweat.

In the end, the girl took pity and told him her name was Molly, invited him back to her flat in Bethnal Green. Her audacity took him aback. It felt, he wrote, like something that happened to other people. He'd heard all the stories from acquaintances who played the local circuit. If you were a muso and half-way decent-looking, he'd heard you were virtually guaranteed at least a knee-trembler around the back of the venue. But that wasn't who he was. He'd been raised to respect women.

While she emptied the stall, he stood, hypnotised at first by the loose leaves and bright petals floating in the buckets of water around her. She brought some of the flowers with her when he offered to pay for a taxi to ferry them across London. He hated being on the streets at any time, but particularly at dusk; a cab would deliver them straight to her door.

The skies had turned a bruised purple. In the concrete car parks of pubs, locals lounged around their cars, the doors open, pints of beer balanced on the bonnets. Their voices carried through the taxi's open windows. Danny was intoxicated by the smell of flowers between Molly's legs, and the way she'd slid her shoes off until they were hanging from her toes. But he couldn't look her in the eye or speak. His mind was a blank.

"It was one of those anonymous East End terraced streets," he wrote. "Concrete gardens. Children playing in the road. A chip shop at one end, an off-license at the other. It was the kind of place you'd never find twice."

Her bedsit, lit with a dull yellow bulb, was already crowded with flowers in vases and cracked tumblers. "I can't just chuck them out," she said in her defence, as if they were lodgers. "All these pretty delphiniums and forget-me-nots."

Danny felt as if they'd arrived for parts in a play for which they had no lines, but then Danny *always* felt that way. Molly made tea for them, which passed some time. Then hesitantly, over the kettle, she said, "Would you like to smoke a joint?"

The way she said it made him laugh, and it seemed to break the ice somewhat. Delighted by the smile on his face, she took him back outside: up the road to the off-license for twenty Embassy, a pack of Rizla papers, and a bottle of cheap wine that would sit in her fridge long after she was dead. Danny's softened demeanour drew Molly out of herself. He felt her hand brushing his fingers as she spoke breathlessly about the little village in Yorkshire where she'd been born, and her sisters who'd spread out through England, eager to be away. Danny didn't discover why, for as they left the shop, Molly's smile stiffened suddenly on her face, and he caught sight of a figure across the street, hovering outside the glow of a streetlamp, beside a rusted Anglia. He unclasped his hands and regarded them solemnly. It was a movement that Danny felt he'd just missed the extent of, and the sudden furtive gesture further into the darkness seemed to confirm it. The memory of the street magician in Leicester Square who'd folded the air bloomed in Danny's mind. He registered dully that Molly had taken hold of his hand and was dragging him back up the street. She looked as apprehensive as he felt. But when Danny peered back into the dusk between the pools of streetlamp light, he could only see a shape easing itself into the car. The engine started, but it didn't pull away. Danny couldn't decide what had just happened, but the stump of his arm was aching. He saw the train emerging from the tunnel of his mind as Molly fumbled nervously with her keys.

He tried inadequately to draw her out afterwards, but as she sat cross-legged on the bed, rolling the joints, her hair tumbling over her eyes, the stiff expression of concentration on her face seemed impenetrable. The bright bloom of her earlier exuberance seemed to have vanished entirely.

They smoked for a while in silence, black hash – eight quid an ounce, she told him – but the sense of closeness that had threatened to blossom between them had receded. Molly's eyes looked barren, he wrote; resolved somehow. "Like someone who'd just had bad news from the hospital." Danny had no idea what to do or say. But after an hour or so, a little bit stoned, she made her first tentative inroads toward him. He resisted initially, of course, as if he were some middle-class twit being propositioned by a socialist: it was in his breeding. Shyly she slid her sweater off. Her body, moving through the fabric, stirred something within him that seemed beyond resisting. "I can protect you," she said, covering his sallow neck in breath and kisses. Slow, drowsy circles with her hands. "If you want me to."

The words made no sense but Danny felt curiously liberated. She opened a window to air the room a little from the smoke. As the breeze made goose-pimples on her skin, they both smiled at each other again, the fear of the events in the street diminishing. In the languid summer silence, he felt an exhilarating vertiginous delight in the way it progressed; their bodies releasing him in a way that words could not.

When she pulled him down beside her, every moment he'd ever had seemed to coalesce. He heard a sudden rain shower begin beyond the window, and when he looked, the sky had suddenly gone black. Starless and bible-black. It seemed to swell in the frame, as if wanting to reach in to them. The light from the bare yellow bulb surged and dimmed, surged and dimmed. In that moment, Danny wrote, Molly was transformed the way dust or rain is when sunlight catches it. He could feel every detail of her, combined and beatific, and he was drunk on it – the realness of her: the flush in her cheeks and throat and breasts; the painted red fingernails, chipped and bitten to the quick; the way her patent leather shoes had rubbed the skin on her ankles red; the wet heat that she fumbled his shaking fingers into. Briefly he saw a glimpse of her life: the gap-toothed girl she'd surely once been in school photographs; the child with a bucket and spade on the beach in Blackpool; the dead-eyed teenager beside a hospital bed, clutching her mother's hand; her body entwined with another girl's in a field by a grey church...

Danny thought it was over, but then there

was more, more life than Molly could feasibly have lived: he saw her old and weathered, but unmistakably her, in a nondescript backyard, with two small children on either side of her (he could hear them saying "Cheese!" brightly, then scampering away); he saw her, ten years from that moment, loading supermarket bags into the back of her car; putting on glasses to tend to the crocuses in her pretty little garden; queuing for lottery tickets, wearing a headscarf and an overcoat...

The moment was too much. Danny couldn't decide if she was more or less than human. Clearly, nothing leading up to this point had been accidental. Molly was unfolding her hands, crying out to the darkness: "You can *fuck off!* Leave us alone!" And then, urgently, to Danny: "Do it now. *Fuck me.* Do it now. *Go on.*"

She led him clumsily inside her. Danny could hardly move. He looked away from her eyes; her gaze seemed to see into him, and he was afraid how little there was to find. Her face was drained of joy. He pressed his own face into her neck, feeling surplus to requirements. He felt sick and alone when he came, and withdrew immediately, assuming the act over.

The breeze from the open window dried the film of sweat from his body while he removed his trousers, which were tangled around his ankles. When he turned back to Molly, she was reaching out for him, pushing her fingers through his hair, and the look on her face hovered between sadness and fondness. The light had gone from the room, the swollen darkness from the window.

"Protect *me* now," she demanded, closing her wrists together and raising her clasped hands to her chest. The gesture was unselfconscious, pure sudden need. Her resolve had gone, he realised. But as much as he wanted to grant her this last request, it was a final gulf that Danny could not cross, despite what she might have given him. "I simply hadn't the strength for two," he wrote.

~ 4 ~

Danny woke to the sound of buses lumbering up Bethnal Green Road, birds singing, the milkman making his rounds. When he reached out expectantly, he found the bed empty. The sheets were drenched with blood.

There was a dreadful resolve to his initial movements, though his ears were ringing with fear. The trail of blood led down off the far side of the bed and around the room, like manic dance steps. The open window couldn't quell the smell of it sufficiently. The flowers had all died. The pale shape at the corner of his vision seemed to swarm, beckon his gaze. Danny said her name, and his voice sounded like a sudden intrusion on the stillness of the room. The absolute quiet seemed to have infected the streets outside, as if all of its components – the buses, the birds, the milkman – were waiting for his next move.

When he finally crossed the room and forced himself to acknowledge Molly, he felt his throat tightening. The edges of his mind were beginning to fray dangerously. Now he had set eyes on her, he couldn't avert his gaze. I imagined him, an obscure folk singer without his trousers, lost in a situation he had no understanding of. It was as if she had turned to porcelain. Her skin was pale and unblemished against the carpet of blood beneath her. He wanted to gather her up into his skinny arms but he was afraid to do so.

He thought of the magician they'd seen on the street. He imagined the figure folding air, moving lightly up the stairs or travelling on the swollen black through the window, silent as a ballerina; opening her up with his bare hands, feeding on all of her lives until there was nothing that remained.

Danny felt abandoned. Molly was in the room, yet she was not. There was only a body and its meagre belongings: clothes, paperbacks, some dusty vinyl, towels on a chair by the fire, a box of tampons on the sink, an ashtray filled with curled joints. The memory of all her lives kept flashing in front of him. He couldn't decide on the truth of things. All he knew for sure was that she had been murdered because of him. It was too much for his fragile state of mind.

Danny retrieved his clothes and fled downstairs, stared at the payphone in the hall for a moment, then picked it up with the intention of alerting the police. But the dead sound that he pressed to his ear made him feel transparent; the voice, when it came, sounded like something huge and made of blackness, reaching up, out of the depths.

Sarah and I watched Andrew from the touchlines as the light faded and the little floodlamps in the park came on. In the still evening air, they drew long, lazy shadows from the players – thin-legged boys with skinned knees and muddy faces. A smattering of parents hollered and whistled from the sidelines, clutching bottles of Evian or cappuccinos from the Starbucks across the street. I saw my ex-wife, and waved.

By the time we'd sold the house and the divorce was finalised, Deborah had found a little place in Sevenoaks for herself and our son, Andrew. We'd had him quite late in life (I was 55 at the time, Deborah 42), and the changed circumstance of that, combined with other less specific things, pushed us away from one another. I never found the perspective that children were supposed to give you. Like Sarah's divorce, it turned out to be a little too amicable, a little too clean. In panic, I'd imagined that the weight of our past, all the assorted ups and downs and photo albums full of our lives together might solve our problems – look at what we've done! How much we've gone through! But it hadn't been that way at all. It was like pulling at one thread that unravels everything. For Deborah it seemed to be a relief to finally let go.

She came over after the game to give Sarah a cursory inspection, and then took Andrew off home in her new husband's Audi. Waving, I watched the taillights vanish, saw the remainder of the evening light exhaust itself entirely. Sarah had barely managed to acknowledge my son or my ex-wife. Daniel's letters had disturbed her. I'd had no intention of keeping them from her; we were together too often in any case: she had underwear in my drawers by this time, a toothbrush and make-up in the bathroom, tights drying on the radiators. I was determined to be as open as possible, even though I knew the letters would upset her. She was already lost in 1976.

On the way home she eventually said, "He phoned me from a station. Monument or Bank – I can't recall. He could hardly speak. I mean it was bloody ridiculous, but I knew it was Danny. I managed to discover where he was and I said I'd be there as soon as possible. I was his breakdown service. So absolutely *absurd*. But there it was. That was my duty as his big sister. When I found him, he was in one of the pedestrian tunnels, sitting on his coat with his guitar in his hand. He looked utterly bewildered."

Sarah stopped in the street, hesitated with the words that she wanted to say. I remained silent; heard the clatter of plates carry from an open kitchen window, watched as lights came on in houses and a high-rise nearby, watched as light flared from the cigarette that Sarah lit while she looked inside herself and then finally back to me.

"I felt awful," she said. "Like there was something I could have done for him before it got to that point."

I took her hands. "You couldn't reach him," I said. "We all tried at some time or another. But people have to want to be helped, and I don't think he did."

She nodded. "That was the nature of his illness. I see that now, but how could he have possibly known what he wanted, what was best for him? I've read all those articles people have written about him in the music press and

Sunday supplements; they seem to think he was born wearing black and listening to bloody Leonard Cohen. But we had a lovely childhood. You *know* that. We were well off, we had a Labrador that Danny adored, family holidays abroad; Mum and Dad put us through public school, university; plenty of friends. We were fine. And then we were so terribly pleased when he got that recording contract with Island Records.

"But it was London. *Bloody London.* Somehow once it got hold of him, it was, I don't know, *corrosive,* somehow. And those last few years, he got away from me. I let him, I suppose. Sometimes it's only the distance that saves us. He always managed to make people feel somehow accountable for all of his feelings, but he nurtured that in me most, you know – *look* what you let me do! Why didn't you *look after* me?

"But anyway, seeing him there with his guitar, I *did* feel ashamed. I helped him into a gent's loo, where he retched into a urinal. He had no weight on him. My hands just closed around his arms. I could feel his ribs through his pullover. And then I found the cigarette burns on the stump of his arm. I went through the roof.

'*Look at this,*' I said. 'What the *bloody hell* do you call this, Daniel? But he didn't care. I don't think he was even listening.

"We ended up on a platform and when he did start talking, he sounded *so* confused. I just thought it was the medication. He was insistent that we shouldn't go out of the Underground, so I bought him a sandwich and he ate a bit of it on a bench with all these people running past. 'They killed her,' he kept saying, but he wouldn't specify who. 'Just a girl. Just a girl.' He was terrified that he'd be accused – that someone might have witnessed him speaking to this girl, or that the taxi driver who took him to Bethnal Green would come forward and identify him. I bought some newspapers and couldn't find anything. I suggested that perhaps she hadn't been found, but it didn't pacify him. He kept telling me things about her, or about other women. He couldn't seem to decide if they were all the same person. But he kept repeating these very specific details. It was like he couldn't keep them all square in his mind. There was just *too much*. I didn't know what to believe.

"Eventually he was so exhausted I managed to get him on a train and back to my flat. I slept on the couch. He didn't ask why everything was in boxes, why my bags were all packed. I suppose he'd suspected it would happen eventually. I knew he would be terribly lonely in London without me here, but I *had* to leave. After you and I split up, I felt weepy and depressed all of the time, and I realised that I had to be stronger than that. Otherwise you just make a vicious circle of your life.

"But I woke up in the middle of the night, and Danny was knelt beside me, stroking my hair. He stared at me until I had to sit up. That was such a *huge* gesture for Danny. I think perhaps he was fearful for me after what he'd imagined had happened to that girl. I was so touched that I tried to reach out to him, put my arms around him, but that seemed to break the spell. He retreated back into himself, and he didn't speak to me after that; not even in the morning when I told him I was leaving London. 'How can I bloody-well help you when you never *talk* to me?' That was the last thing I ever said to him."

Sarah didn't offer anything else all the rest of the way home. She'd talked herself into some sad, regretful place. I tried to draw her out of it, change the subject, but she'd retreated just as

Danny had. She seemed more pacified by my arms around her in bed than by anything I could say.

During the night, I woke to find her gone. After all we'd spoken about, I felt a panic rise in me. Halfway down the staircase, I heard her voice: she was speaking quietly to someone in the kitchen. When she said Danny's name, the jolt of fear made me stumble downwards, two, three steps at a time. Until that point I had seen the letters and my life as separate entities. Perhaps I had been ignorant.

When I reached the kitchen however, I found Sarah asleep at the breakfast table. I touched her hair, and the panic subsided to something softer, more affectionate. I felt ridiculous, easily alarmed; suddenly terribly *old*. Perhaps she had been talking in her sleep. But as I considered waking her, I heard an abrupt frenzied scrabbling outside, and then a panting, like breathless dogs fighting. I realised the back door was ajar.

Without thinking, I crossed the kitchen quickly and stepped outside in my bare feet. But without my glasses, the back yard could have had my son's football team in it and I wouldn't have seen them. All I could hear by that time was the washing flapping stiffly in the breeze, the sound of taxis idling streets away. My mind kept leading me back to folding hands and young girls with multiple lives. I locked the door, checked the windows, and then woke Sarah, who was only disorientated to find herself sleeping at the kitchen table. We went back to bed.

Perhaps I should have made more sense of things there and then, made some correlation, however ridiculous. But I didn't.

~ 6 ~

After leaving Sarah's flat in Battersea, Danny rode the Underground, criss-crossing lines throughout central London. There was a pull in him by now that was distorting his thoughts. His memory failed him. He felt bereaved and couldn't recall why. But he knew somehow that he was stumbling around the precipice of the truth.

Somehow he made it back to his place in Haverstock Hill, which was across the road from the entrance to Chalk Farm tube station. I remember his flat purely by the paucity of his belongings. He lived like a squatter. It was a back room away from the street, huge French windows overlooking the gardens. The sun rose through them in the morning. As it crept along the bare wooden floorboards that morning, Danny destroyed everything systematically: the record player and the collection of vinyl; his small-bodied Guild guitar; his reel to reel for demos; the print of the cover of his debut album, framed on the wall; the faded Penguin paperbacks, mouldering beneath the window. "I hated it all," he wrote. "None of it had anything to do with what remained of my life."

Afterwards, breathless and sated, he swallowed some of his prescription drugs with tap water, drew the curtains and lay down on the mattress, imaging that Molly was beside him.

He woke on another crowded tube train. For a brief moment he was as disorientated as ever. The compartment was so full that he couldn't rise from the seat he found himself in. When he tried to catch the eyes of the other passengers, their faces were all somehow turned away.

Danny felt a surge of paranoia. Blind panic set in.

The train slowed, sighed to a halt. The doors hissed open. No one moved. Danny struggled to get out of his seat again, but the bodies around him were as rigid as stone. He was too reserved to raise his voice to the unyielding throng, so he acquiesced. He craned his neck in order to see which station they'd alighted at, but the platform was unlit, deserted. He could smell earth through the open doors, he wrote, the rich scent of freshly dug soil; and he knew then, as the doors closed and the train lurched forward, that he was finally being led to whatever it was that had plagued him all this time.

The conclusion gave him strength and he was out of his seat, fumbling through the cluster of passengers. He felt no air of anticipation in the crowd, no fear; nothing at all. When he came face to face with one of them, it was like looking at a mask. The eyes were vacant, utterly detached. It was the very least that a face could be. "I wondered," Danny wrote, "if it saw the same in me. But how could it? The rest of them seemed to be complicit in their inactivity, their silence."

When the train began to slow again, Danny unthreaded himself from the throng of bodies, and then stepped out onto the platform. When he turned to look back at the open doors, the clustered figures stared blankly back at him. He recognised details finally: raincoats; shopping bags; umbrellas; a child with chocolate around his mouth, still in his pyjamas.

Danny fell back onto a hard plastic bench and curled up, his hand closed over his face. He couldn't think clearly. His head felt leaden, as if he had taken too much of his medication. His limbs were heavy with lethargy.

But still. The smell of fresh earth. "Like after a rain shower," he wrote. He was thinking of the heat of a summer's day, somewhere above him, and the vacated rooms and roads where all of these people should have rightfully been, if their bodies had not been lured away. That pull. The promise of something incomprehensible. They'd felt it too.

Finally Danny rose and watched as the passengers began to disembark in short, jerky motions. They jumped down onto the tracks between the train and the platform. *Mind the gap*, Danny thought. Was this their destination?

A point of no return? He wanted to bolt, but he knew that simply wasn't possible, despite his apparent distinction from the rest of the passengers. And he had to *know*. This was, I suppose, his tree filled with angels.

The passengers were drifting into the next tunnel: a huge, silent procession from the carriages, gradually being enveloped by the dark. Danny hesitated until the train had been entirely vacated. He was reluctant to be in close proximity to the rest of them for fear of losing his autonomy somehow. Pulling his coat tightly around him, he jumped down between the tracks and followed the tail-end of the line into the tunnel, where they became a grey mass. He stretched his undamaged arm out in front of himself, and stumbled blindly forward for some time until the gloom began to glow; gradually the tunnel was opening out into an immense cavern. The temperature had dropped palpably. It took Danny's breath away momentarily; once he'd grasped the sheer size of the cave, astonishment did the same. He couldn't see the ceiling. The slightest sound of movement rose and lingered in the air, echoed for long moments afterwards. "It was like a cathedral," he wrote. Amongst the stalagmite basins and the stalactite pillars, he could hear the sound of something like prayer. He was terrified and in awe.

The crowd was disrobing, casting off their clothes with cold, mechanical efficiency. Danny hovered on the periphery. He could feel an itching in his head to do the same, become part of the mass. The sight of the hand-folders, moving amongst the crowd, gesticulating silently, only made him more fearful of what was to come. Although it was a magic still beyond his comprehension, he had first-hand knowledge of their capabilities. The air was growing restless around them; there were strange phosphorescent seeds, drifting from their hands and through the air, like fireflies. And then they were everywhere, multiplying hypnotically in the gloom before Danny's eyes.

When he heard the dull rumble of trains around him, he looked back at the mouth of the tunnel, but realised that the sound belonged to something else, something vast that was waiting in the darkness: a huge invisible presence that had been invoked. For a brief, devastating moment, Danny and the crowd were delivered to a clear, untouched beach. There were no lights inland, no one at sea; no other signs of life. But in the deafening silence Danny found himself staring up at a sky that seemed too full of stars, and at a darkness that was swiftly eclipsing them: vast shapes like broken satellites, plummeting at astonishing speed, out of the night and into the ocean. The murmurs from the crowd sounded to Danny like massed prayer. Upon impact a colossal tidal wave seemed to rear like a startled animal. It rose, seemingly back into the stars, and froze into an image that folded in upon itself. They were delivered back into the gloom of the cave, left to cower before a giant, impassive presence that had somehow found its way beneath the world: forever in exile, but always exerting its influence. A whisper that found the ears of those who were listening. Something empty calling out to the lost.

Danny felt humbled and terrified, rooted to the moist earth beneath his feet. The crowd had begun to disperse. The seeds floating in the air seemed to multiply again, until their glow made his vision blur. The people were merging and unpeeling, softening. They left pale trails in the air, like images burned on his retinas. As if he'd stared at a light-bulb in an empty room. "The afterbirth of ghosts," Danny wrote. They were coming undone. He could smell the sweet scent of grass after rainfall, or semen on skin, then the heady smell of wildflowers on a summer evening. Molly's face came unbidden to his mind, like a light to follow. Danny realised then that he could feel the shapes that the crowd had metamorphosed into; they were turbulent portraits of lives too vast and beautiful and angry to be contained, but offered up for consumption to the hungry darkness. At Danny's sudden realisation, the presence heaved and he felt a rush of vertigo as the soil loosened beneath his feet. There were seeds in his mouth; they tasted of salt and raw eggs as they slid down the back of his throat. His mind loosened until he was screaming against the diminishing crowd's prayer. Then he was floundering away from it all, stumbling through the cast-off clothes, somehow spared.

As Danny bolted back into the tunnel, he could only think of Molly and her memories: all those lives. Somehow, with every step, they were peeling away from him: the school photos, the teenager by the bed, the couple in the field, the old woman in the backyard and loading bags into her car, tending crocuses, a multitude more... until all that remained was the shell of her memory. It was the sacrifice that let him leave, he believed; but somewhere between the dark and the light, Danny came essentially to the end of his own life. He wrote this without a trace of self-pity or loss.

When he woke in the familiar surroundings of the psychiatric hospital that he'd only left a few months previously, he cursed Molly for sparing him. Everything was the same: the blanket of medication; the sad, vapid stares; the moments of sheer claustrophobia and unbridled panic; even the girl with the smile in the waiting room, still pissing herself after all this time. I visited him once, and he spent most of the time asking me about Sarah, but when she had left London, we had simply lost touch in those intervening years.

It was 1977 when he was released. Winter edging tentatively into spring. He loathed the diminished winter days. Dark by four p.m. He went down to the nearest tube station, but something had changed. "I no longer felt the pull," he wrote. Something was gone or had never been there at all. Sometimes he looked for Molly, sensing that she was no longer a corpse in a Bethnal Green bedsit, but was probably back selling flowers somewhere. He couldn't find her either. Deep in his damaged mind, he felt an acute sense of loss; like finding that someone no longer loved you enough to keep you.

It was as if there were no more pertinent years in Danny's life. He popped up from time to time, of course. Various people would say that they'd spotted him in hostels, homeless shelters, subways at dusk, or hanging around his old studio in Chelsea. Apocryphal tales of his playing some notes of piano on someone's record, singing in a club with a young man purported to be his lover, playing guitar. Eventually his record company released an album of songs he'd been working on before his suicide attempt, and bookended it with demos and live recordings. That and his debut record have stayed on the Island catalogue ever since. There was enough residual affection and respect for him to become a myth to journalists and photographers in the music press; a cult artist. But there were no more letters.

After much deliberation, Sarah and I moved in together. Our money stretched to buying a two-bedroom terrace in Primrose Hill, despite the fact that I had wanted to move from London altogether. Sarah decorated it in pastel shades, and we bought new furniture to fill it with. Even though she'd been retired for a few years she found herself a part-time nursing job in a psychiatric unit just three miles down the road. My son, Andrew, stayed every other weekend. He helped us pick a sad-eyed mongrel from the Battersea pound; we called her Lola. I wrapped the letters from Danny in an elastic band, hid them in a drawer upstairs, and pretended to forget about them. We were cautiously happy.

Then one day, six months after Danny's last missive, I arrived home to find Sarah gone. I phoned the hospital. The sister in charge said she hadn't been in work for the past week. I tried her mobile. No answer. When I woke the following morning alone, I alerted the police, and stayed in for the first few days, expecting her to walk through the door as if nothing untoward had happened. When that didn't happen, instinctively I went out and down into the Underground, and travelled most of the lines for much of that day and the next. Half of me expected to stumble upon her, looking perplexed and dishevelled on a platform bench, but I didn't. I re-read Danny's letters eventually, trying to find something, some path he had taken that I could re-tread some forty-odd years on. Read without the comfort of scepticism, they simply terrified me. And I realised too that perhaps he had known that whatever was down there was exerting its influence again, calling somehow.

I remembered Sarah telling me how she had woken that last night with Danny stroking her hair protectively, and I realised then that the letters had never really been intended for me. They had been written at the time as a warning, but Sarah had left London and saved herself. I imagined Danny on the periphery of our lives, trying to protect us; somehow he'd known that his sister had returned, and had felt that similar pull. Perhaps he'd thought that those old letters might still stave off the dark as Molly's lives had. But whatever their purpose, Sarah and I had failed to see them for what they were. How could we?

I often went down to the Underground in the subsequent weeks, each time with my hope a little more diminished. Nothing redeemed me, not even the days when my son visited. I was bereft. I travelled aimlessly beneath London, often finding myself there at ten or eleven at night; an old man poring over the tube map, trying to plot my way back onto the Northern Line, or else sitting on platforms, staring vacantly. Once I had accepted that she was gone, I wanted to feel a similar pull in me, feel my body luring me away from this world. I started looking into the shadows for indistinct figures with their hands folding air, or a flower-seller with lives to give away.

Instead I would reach our home, exhausted and empty, feed the dog, turn lights on and off, push Sarah's clothes to my face and inhale, and then lie awake all night. Sometimes I'd drift off and wake up bewildered in the small hours and find her side of the bed empty, stumble downstairs and expect to find her asleep at the kitchen table with the back door ajar. But it was the wrong house, and I realised eventually that it was too late in life to continue feeling that way: waiting for the rug to be pulled, moving in circles; lost and found, lost and found.

Eventually, after making the decision to move away from London, I put the house back on the market. I spent several weeks wrestling with despair and indecision. Too much paperwork and too many details to finalise. I hated the nights most. I hated telling Andrew that I'd not see him as often. I had to reassure myself that I was not simply fleeing. My ex-wife never said as much, but I think she assumed I was making a drama out of the whole situation: that Sarah had simply wised up to me and buggered off back to Birmingham. Still, who knew the truth? A mad, washed-up folk singer in his seventies, living rough? Perhaps, but I kept hearing Sarah saying sometimes it's only distance that saves us. So I sold everything that she and I had bought, put the rest of it in the car, and Lola in the passenger seat, and drove away one morning. I held Sarah in my mind for a while. Then at some point, many miles beyond London, I realised what I was doing, and let distance and time take her away from me forever.

Perfidious
Albion

~ 1 ~

"This is all there is, I'm afraid," the nurse said, handing me the box. George's room was now bare. The bed stripped of its sheets. The bookcases empty. His chair beside the window vacant, his impression still evident in the cushions. The leaves were falling beyond the window, quickly now; we were in October's suddenly frigid clutches. It had enveloped the days, necessitating scarfs and coats and premature cold medicine. Britain was never ready to relinquish summer, always unprepared for plummeting temperatures. I took the box from the nurse and glanced inside. The sudden surge of emotion at the absolute inadequacy of its contents seemed to swell from deep within me and close my throat. The nurse smiled at me with that practised look of sympathy nurses develop from being exposed to all kinds of grief; she closed a chilly hand around mine. Her name was Virginia. She'd been here at the residential care home for years. Over that time I'd seen the grey gradually creep from the roots of her hair and steal the colour away entirely. She was almost always at the home when I visited; she was one of George's favourites despite his inability to properly display any kind of gratitude. George had suffered from what the doctors called dissociative fugue, amnesia and schizophrenia. Some days you would arrive to find him quite upbeat, sitting out in the grounds in his bright scarf with his thick grey hair tied back in a rough ponytail, listening to the football results, and you'd be convinced that this was the brother you'd had as a child and that nothing awful had ever befallen him. But then there were other days where you would discover him in his room at the window, mute, his hair loose over his bereft face, utterly disconnected from the world and who he was. Unreachable.

A week ago George had made his fourth escape from the care home. He'd caught a bus from Bath towards Glastonbury. He'd always gone back that way, but was usually intercepted by someone from the hospital or the local authorities before he came to harm. This time had been different. This time, before he reached Glastonbury, he stumbled onto some train tracks and fell under an oncoming train.

The last time I'd seen George was when our old man died. Virginia had accompanied my brother to the funeral and he'd stood stiffly in his cheap suit with his hands clasped behind his back, his face quite empty. When I talked to him afterwards it was as if we'd bumped into each other in the supermarket:

"Oh! Hello, how are you?"

"Bearing up, I suppose. How are you, George? You look well."

"Oh, you know. Gosh! Can't complain. They're treating me as well as can be expected."

It was like talking to someone from the Famous Five. Afterwards Virginia drove him away in a little Fiat Punto, back to the residential home in Perrymead, away from people who could hurt him, or vice versa. He waved at me as they pulled away and he was briefly my big brother again on the day he moved out of the house, his Ford Escort piled high with seventeen years-worth of shit in the back.

George's talents suggested great things for him, but by the tail-end of the eighties he was all but lost to us, as well as to himself. His already fragile mind swallowed up and spat out. The other side of that event necessitated him spending most of his adult life in institutions like this one. George had never spoken a word about those years, so there were gaps that we'd never properly filled. Lost time.

And now George was gone and all that was left was this box. And in that box, beside a framed photograph of the family and some dog-eared paperbacks was a videotape. And on that videotape was scrawled 'PERFIDIOUS ALBION'.

~ **2** ~

That night I drove back to Dorset. This wasn't home anymore. My old man had kept the lights burning in this rough Dorset house for years after my mum had died. Even after they'd found George, my parents had taken him back in and tended to their adult son as if he was still a child. This house with its views of the Jurassic Coast was the story of our lives. And so I couldn't let it go, even though that made the most sense. I kept putting distance between myself and this place but it kept calling me back. The past still had a hold on me.

I'd been provided with a consent form and the care home had assisted with local funeral directors and registering the death. But I knew the drill by now. I'd made arrangements for my parents' funerals, and for other relatives. That not-so-gentle surety of mortality as you danced around fifty. Your loved ones falling ill, losing their minds and memories while you sat with them, waiting for the inevitable, sometimes hoping for it to come faster, if only to release them from their suffering and to release you from the ponderous calamity of death. So I made the calls just as the funeral directors was closing and arranged to go down there the next morning to talk about what I wanted for my brother.

I sat down at the kitchen table in my more or less empty family home and traced my fingers against the scratches and whorls of the wood, intimately familiar with each of them. The marks that George and I had scratched there when we were kids, acutely aware of the scolding we'd get from Mum or Dad when they noticed. After the old man passed and I'd bagged up all of the things that needed to be removed from the house, I'd decided I couldn't part with this table. Even now, sitting here in a cold house that I should have put on the market a couple of years ago, I could feel the history of my family in the grain of the wood and in the stone underfoot, the rug beside the fire, the sofa where we'd sat watching TV on a Saturday night. Getting rid of these things doesn't divest you of your memories, but these objects have a hold on us; they're like time machines or ouija boards, offering an intoxicating approximation of all the things you've lost. The faintest glimmer of ghosts.

The old man's TV had a VCR under it, gathering dust but still working. I took the videotape out of the box of George's possessions and slipped it into the slot. Without thinking, I slumped back into the spot on the sofa I'd always sat in when I was a kid, pressed PLAY on the remote control.

Watching something on VHS is its own type of time machine in its way. Snatches of some lost TV show from the eighties taped for posterity then taped over; snippets of old adverts you thought you'd forgotten, the quality so poor you can scarcely believe we could watch and enjoy them. I watched for five faintly nostalgic minutes or so before I started fast-forwarding. There was a long spell of static and I thought that there might be nothing else, that I'd gotten invested in something that proved to be nothing at all. But then, just as I was about to stop the tape, the static blistered and revealed something beneath. Like an ancient artefact a title card read: PLAY FOR TODAY, and then: PERFIDIOUS ALBION.

After he'd left home, one of our uncles who lived in London, a rather theatrical man with what my mother quietly referred to at the time as his 'gentleman lodgers', had managed to get George a job in the production offices of the BBC drama department. My brother would return during the summer and at Christmas with fantastic stories from Television Centre in Shepherd's Bush. Thousands of people worked there every day. George would regale us over a kitchen table festooned with crackers and turkey about wheeling Daleks around the studios while Tom Baker tripped over his scarf; and then one day how he'd literally walked into David Bowie, who happened to be leaving the Old Grey Whistle Test studios. "Look where you're going, mate." George treasured those words from a testy rock legend, and so did I. In the new year I told all my mates when we went back to school that my brother was rubbing shoulders with the greats: *Baker and Bowie.* He talked about making contacts with a young producer called Malcolm, who'd expressed an interest in his ideas at a party. George's new life sounded breathlessly exciting to a fourteen year old who missed his brother more than he could admit to anyone.

He moved up to Birmingham a couple of years later to direct a couple of episodes of 'Gangsters,' and then to begin production on 'Perfidious Albion,' a *Play for Today.* Some of the initial work was being produced at Pebble Mill studios in Edgbaston, which, in the seventies, was a formidable outpost of BBC Drama. Before deregulation, television dramas had a greater focus on reflecting life in Britain, and *Play for Today* had a reputation for social and political radicalism, and a distinct willingness to provoke controversy. This freedom had attracted writers and directors such as Dennis Potter, Ingmar Bergman, Alan Clarke and Ken Loach, as well as a host of new talent who could hone their skills on rare, much coveted slots for plays shot on 16 mm film.

George had been waiting patiently for his opportunity. He'd been honing his script for 'Perfidious Albion' for years, and in Birmingham he found the freedom to experiment with different styles of storytelling. He was still only twenty years old. It was a ridiculous opportunity for someone so young, but George's talent was as prodigious as his imagination. We didn't see him very often during this period, just the occasional phone call to keep my mother apprised of his living conditions and overall health. My parents offered to drive up to Birmingham to visit him more than once, but George told them he was far too busy with the production of his play. I didn't speak to him at all. I was 16 at that point, going through the same growing pains that George had at that age; awkward and withdrawn and given to solitude. I didn't want to speak to anyone, let alone my family. Consequently we knew precious little about 'Perfidious Albion'. We had to wait until it was shown on television in 1979. The old man insisted I come downstairs and watch it, which I did with some reluctance.

I could tell afterwards that my parents were bemused by the play. We didn't talk about it afterwards. I retreated back upstairs, my head swarming with the images that my brother had conjured onto film. It followed me into sleep like a degraded analogue signal, transmitting images of Joseph of Arimathea's staff, rooting in the Somerset earth and flowering in crude animation; the terraces of Glastonbury Tor splitting open to reveal another world within; the bombast of William Blake's Jerusalem: its holy lamb of God, its dark satanic mills, chariots of fire and green and pleasant land pacing me through my restless sleep. I'll tell you this: it dogged me, George's play. It dogged me for years. It whispered things to me that only I would know; peeled away secrets and suggested truths that hardened into tenets that I based my life on. I never saw it again.

I'd hoped that this innocuous videotape would open that world up again for me. My memory was hazy by now. Only core images remained, burned into my life; they followed me into sleep even now, those increasingly degraded signals, still transmitting like the shipping forecast on an old radio. But all that remained of 'Perfidious Albion' on that tape of George's were the first ten minutes. I sat in my parent's old house with the evening spread out across the sky and my broken heart lifting out of my body towards my dead brother and his lost film.

Those first ten minutes still burned brightly:

Joseph of Arimathea and Nicodemus, washing the bloodied body of Christ, collecting two drops of blood from Jesus's side in the cup from the Last Supper, then wrapping him in linen and placing him a sepulchre cut out of rock. Joseph the missionary, fleeing Palestine, sailing through storms and, upon arriving in Glastonbury, fixing his pilgrim's staff in the ground at Wearyall Hill. The day accelerating into night and back into day as the staff flowers into a blossoming thorn tree. Joseph burying the Grail at the foot of Glastonbury Tor, whereupon a spring of blood gushes from the ground. Night and day and clouds and storms hasten across the sky. Jerusalem stirs. When the camera returns to the base of the Tor, a teenage boy in modern clothes is clambering though the weathered terraces, as if following an ancient magical pattern...

At that point the music began to whine and go out of tune. The picture shattered and static rolled up across the screen as the tape's magnetic oxide flaked away on the VCR's heads. I fast forwarded the tape and pressed PLAY, hoping to locate the remainder of 'Perfidious Albion,' but all that existed was that ten precious minutes of footage. I watched it again, and then, sensing it degrading in the video recorder, ejected the tape. Suddenly it became a precious artefact; a crucial piece of my family's history.

Nine years after making the film, the police found George wandering along a narrow B-road on a cold January evening, five miles out of Glastonbury. My parents drove that night to the police station where they were holding George. Their initial relief faded when they discovered that my brother was being transferred to a nearby hospital for a psychiatric examination. Aside from some indication of malnutrition, he showed no physical signs of mistreatment. But my mother was horrified after spending an hour with him. "It's like he's just not there anymore," she told me on the phone the next morning. "It's like someone has stolen his personality away from him."

The doctors found drugs in his system. Psilocybin mushrooms and LSD. They came to the conclusion that George had had one bad trip too many. I remembered reading about the same thing happening to Syd Barret from Pink Floyd, and Peter Green from Fleetwood Mac. Their subsequent years lost to psychedelic drugs too powerful to control.

I realised that I'd been staring at the static on my old man's TV set long enough for the sky to have darkened outside the windows. A storm had crept across the Jurassic Coast and was picking up dead leaves and branches, and hurling them against the windows. Mum always used to say that George had been born during a storm, and ever since, that storm had followed him around. After they found him she was convinced that that storm had moved inside him during those absent years and stolen him away from us.

Born in a storm. I unpacked my bags, I locked

the doors and closed the curtains and then crawled into bed while it raged outside.

~ 3 ~

When I was young I followed George everywhere. There were four years between us. When we were kids he'd take me camping in the woodland on the Isle of Purbeck, or on a day trip down to Weymouth. He knew a little bit about everything. He read about mythology and history and nature; he took me looking for sand lizards and smooth snakes and ladybird spiders on the Dorset heathlands. He told me that the chalk giant etched into a hill in Cerne Abbas was a viking who raided the English coast before falling asleep on the hill, and that sometimes he rose from the dead to quench his thirst in the local stream. I lapped it up, tall stories and all. But gradually the relationship changed. By the time he reached fifteen George was changing, struggling with adolescence; with things he seemed incapable of sharing with anyone, let alone me. He wrote voraciously during this time, and watched obscure films that showed on BBC2 late at night, after everyone had gone to bed. He was planting the first seeds that would grow into 'Perfidious Albion.'

The last time George ever took me anywhere I was twelve and he was 16. By that age his face was riddled with acne. He'd grown his hair long, partly in reverence for his musical heroes, but also to hide behind. He had made friends with some people who lived in Glastonbury, and when my old man discovered that George had been invited up there for the weekend he insisted that my brother take me with him. No matter how wayward George had become, my old man knew my presence would ensure that nothing untoward happened with this new crowd. We may have drifted apart but I was still George's little brother. The old man was magnanimous enough to believe George wouldn't run with the wrong crowd. He was wrong. He should have just said no.

The new friend called himself Aesop. He rented a flat above a taxidermist shop on the high street. There were Indian cloths draped everywhere. Incense and marijuana smoke filled the air, a deeply unfamiliar and heady scent that made me light-headed. There were rugs and cushions on the floor, statues of Buddha and

Hindu gods. The gentle sound of wind chimes and John Martyn on the stereo. Although it was only midday there were young people congregated on the steps outside and slumped in the bathroom and kitchen and all down the narrow hall. It was a rich, dark womb of a flat. A subculture in microcosm. It swallowed you whole. I could feel George gripping my shoulder as we navigated our way towards the focal point of all this activity. Aesop had blond hair, pale green eyes, a loose white shirt and grubby looking jeans. Bare feet. He was seated beside a small window, bathed in midsummer sun. He looked like a messiah; he'd freely cultivated the look, fostered the notion in the people who came here to smoke weed and drop acid and listen to his declarations and postulations, as if a 26-year-old man could open the world up for them so they could slip in and drop out.

I don't know how George came to meet Aesop. People were swept up into his orbit somehow; he had some strange quirk of magnetic personality and charisma that attracted a certain kind of soul: a little bit lost, isolated from others, but harbouring suspicions that the world was not composed of the staid conservative values that their parents had instilled in them. He stood to embrace George and then turned his attention to me.

"So who do we have here?"

"My brother," George said, his sullen tone expressing his feelings quite categorically.

"And what brings you here, little seeker?" Aesop asked.

"The bus," I said.

Even at twelve I could spot a cunt when I saw one.

Nonetheless Aesop invited us in to his little coterie that day. He sent someone out for soft drinks for me and for more booze for everyone else. I sat next to a girl who called herself Petal. She smelled of patchouli and cigarettes. She had a distant quality to her that was either the consequence of too much weed or neurological damage. Aesop was expounding about Glastonbury to George:

"It's this supposedly enlightened community, isn't it? That's what they'd have you believe. People spending money on clairvoyants and spiritual courses and all the *woo-woo* crap they sell here. Meanwhile there are all these lost souls, these poor fuckers who wash up here and end up in doorways, drinking themselves into an early grave. It's a fucking sham, this place. *Really*. Lots of divorced women who become landladies, surrounded by cats."

I got bored quite quickly. After an hour or so, George was engaged in an intense conversation with Aesop, who was using a Hawkwind album sleeve to roll up spliffs. I picked my way through the throngs of people. The men were all sour or stoned; the girls giggled and twisted my hair around their fingers. I escaped into what I took to be Aesop's bedroom. There was a mattress on the floor. A thin sheet nailed across the window did nothing to stem the tide of golden Glastonbury sunlight from rushing in. There were maps and drawings and old black and white photographs pinned across the entire expanse of the opposite wall. When I got closer I could see that there was twine leading from one thing to another, gradually causing a huge criss-crossing pattern of (ley) lines of information and enquiry that was almost impossible to divine. There were small notes, signifying references to various key life moments. A map of someone's life. Was Emily there? I suppose so, but all these years after the fact, it's almost impossible to say if she was.

Who's Emily? Wait. I'll get to that.

It must have been the weed in the air; I lay down after a cursory investigation of the wall. When I awoke the light had left the room and I was shrouded in darkness. I could still hear music through the walls; a throbbing sound that made me feel like I'd been swallowed up into a stomach room. After a while I emerged, yawning, my hair awry. It was late in the evening and the faces that greeted me were mostly changed now. A ever-shifting sea of pilgrims, come to touch the hem of Aesop's garment. I was relived to find George, still at Aesop's side. For a moment I imagined he might have abandoned me here in this strange flat in this strange town that in my limited experience was not like anywhere else.

"Religion is ritual," Aesop was saying. "You see? Paganism is celebration. Yeah? Religion is a tool of the state. Paganism is the practice of the people."

I could tell immediately that there was a change in George. He glanced up at me but his gaze was loose and unfocused. His hands distracted him. He waved them in slow motion across his face and smiled. I hadn't seen him smile recently, but this didn't strike me as a particularly welcome development. He got to his feet when he saw me and reached out. I took his hands but I didn't know what to do.

"The time is out of joint, little seeker!" Aesop exclaimed. "Take your brother and open the door to Avalon." He immediately lost interest in us. We were dismissed.

George stumbled outside. He almost slipped down the stairs. I took hold of him, led my older brother away from the clamour of Aesop's flat and into the night. The moon was huge and pink. I remember that quite clearly, but then again that detail might in retrospect be apocryphal; charging my memories with signs and portents that were never really there. It feels like a lifetime ago. Someone called Dave the Sage was waiting for us. Aesop had arranged for us to be driven out to Glastonbury Tor so that George could fulfil what Aesop foresaw as his providence. Dave the Sage was another stoner kid who'd just got his licence and a clapped out VW camper van. It laboured up the narrow streets of the A361, past the Chalice Well where Joseph of Arimathea placed the chalice that had caught the drops of Christ's blood at the Crucifixion, immediately causing the waters to flow red. Had George been of sound mind he would have also pointed out that the iron oxide deposits gave the water a reddish hue, and that the well was a symbol of the female aspect of the deity, with the male symbolised by the Tor. To George mythology and religion and archaeology were all part of the feast that was Albion. We turned up a narrow lane and Dave dropped down to second gear. Sweat beads formed on his brow. But then there was another turn to a single track lane and there it was, draped in pink moonlight, a simple conical hill topped by a gaunt and ruined tower, but somehow far more than that, dressed up in a multitude of layers of fictions that overlapped and lived and breathed in everyone who came here.

Dave the Sage, once parked in a verge at the foot of the Tor, suddenly became loquacious. Aesop had appointed him as our guide. "Can you see the terraces?" he said. "*Carved* terraces. Now, some people say they were created for agricultural stuff a long time ago, but if you ask me, and *you should*, well, I think they're part of an ancient seven-circuit labyrinth."

George tumbled out of the van, his eyes now lucid and his body set with the task ahead.

"What kind of labyrinth?" I asked. I couldn't take my eyes off the hill.

"A Cretan maze, in a meander pattern," Dave said. "Made for spiritual and ritual purposes. You see these terraces, yeah? These terraces circle the Tor seven times and lead you to the entrance of Annwn, the Celtic underworld."

"Like Hell?"

"No mate, like the faery world. But not like you think. They're like ancient Pagan gods. They're bleeding dangerous. You accept the hospitality of the faeries by partaking of their food and drink, and you'll never be able to leave their world again."

"Let's go," George said. "Come on. Just you and me."

George took hold of my wrist and pulled me up the chalk path, rising up along the hill, snaking around it. We walked for what seemed like an eternity. At some point a storm crept across the land and consumed us. The wind began to howl and rain stung our faces. George was mute one moment, loudly euphoric the next, his eyes swimming with things I could not see. His normal sense of self broken down and replaced with a sense of reconnection to himself and the world around him. I could see the red roofs and spires of the town far below us, and the sister hills, Wearyall and Chalice. Hills and rivers and woods becoming less real the higher we climbed. The rain became torrential. Another flood was coming to Avalon.

It was steeper under foot than it had seemed at the base of the hill. I kept slipping in the mud. My coat and my jeans were covered in cow shit. Our shadows sprawled behind us, all the way back down to where Dave sat inside his camper van with a Dion Fortune paperback and a fat spliff. I had been considering Dave's warning about the entrance to Annwn, and the perilousness of the faeries magnanimity. Despite the storm, George was grimly determined. *Born in a storm.* It was nothing to him. I didn't know what had brought him to this acceptance of his fate here in the terraces of Glastonbury Tor. I was no longer privy to his inner or outer life. All I knew for sure was that my older brother was no longer really my friend in the way he had been for so many years. And here on this hill, even though we were together, we were very much apart. I had no idea how to mend that fence. Time would heal that rift, the one that many brothers and sisters go through as they navigate the mine-field of puberty. Everything is a drama at that age; everything is the end of the world. But this actually was. I could feel it coming through the deluge: the end of our world by navigating our way into another one. I suddenly missed my parents and wanted only to run back down the hill, but then who would look after George?

Gradually the storm came to a simmer and a stillness gripped the night by the scruff of the neck. The quality of the air and the light changed. I could feel it, the atmosphere, charging itself up as if preparation for a storm of far more apocalyptic proportions. The sweet pungent zing of ozone in the air, pricking at my nostrils. I could feel the small hairs on the back of my neck standing up. George had stopped smiling, stopped making sense. I felt afraid and alone; at the age of twelve what you believe to be true is not yet hard and fast in your mind.

After following the labyrinth, we arrived, some four hours later, at the ragged grey tower. The pink moon seemed vast, close enough to touch. The sky and all its billions of stars seemed to tilt on an axis, as if the world was suddenly in fast-forward. I could hear music playing over our ragged breaths. Singing in celebration. I was light-headed. I thought for a moment I could see into the world and there, waiting for us, was a strange congregation. There were lights strung from the trees inside the split in the world, men and women dancing and laughing and chasing each other through the flickering firelight. The warm breeze was floral and fragrant.

I could feel a *pull*.

George felt it too. He was like a moth to a flame. This strange fascination stole up on us both. You couldn't help yourself. Their song was creeping into my skull and taking up residence there. George was laughing again, but it wasn't the drugs, it was the intoxication of a better world, just a few steps away, away from the anguish he felt, his deep uncertainty about the world he lived in, and his place in it. I wouldn't understand any of this until I saw 'Perfidious Albion' some years later. Some things can't be said, not even to loved ones. Sometimes you have to let art say it for you, let the audience take it and digest it and own it for themselves.

I didn't see much. I was bewildered and frightened, desperate to be back home in my room, where the world still made sense. But I glimpsed them. They were beautiful. Tall like willow trees. Fine like bee's wings. Like Oberon and Titania, weaving Yeats' unquiet dreams and olden dances, beguiling us away from a world more full of weeping than we could understand.

"George…" I began, intending to cajole him back from this perfection but having nothing to offer other than shared blood. They turned to us then, and I felt my resolve crumble. I stumbled towards them, despite myself. I could feel the warmth of their summer evening on my skin already, could taste their bounty, laid out on tables under the moonlight.

But then I heard my name and it broke the spell somehow. A firm hand on my arm. I didn't know the man. He wasn't familiar but he knew our names. "George," he said in a gentle but firm tone. "Come away now, there's a good lad."

Something changed then. *They* changed. Or I saw them clearly for the first time. The scales falling from my eyes, I saw the sly malice in their enticements. Their bodies stiffened and the fruit corrupted on the vine. They were dwindled gods, just as Dave the Sage had suggested. The stars stilled and the moon was smeared with clouds. I hadn't realised there were tears in my eyes until the man took me in his arms and said, "There we are now. Come away."

George glanced back one more time and then the man took hold of his arm, pulled him close too. George was shaking. The man held him until he stopped and the world was just the world again.

And then we went back to it.

~ 4 ~

We had a short committal ceremony for George in a chapel on the outskirts of Bath. It was a dismal day. It rained on and off that morning as we made our way to the chapel through the wet gardens, already ankle deep with fallen leaves. For a moment I thought it was just going to be me and the minister, but then Virginia arrived in her little Fiat Punto. She looked like a different person in civilian clothes with her hair loose.

"I'm sorry I'm late," she said. "I've just finished my shift. I got changed and came straight here." Her cheeks looked scrubbed and red with the shock of the cold. She took my hands in hers and smiled that reassuring smile.

"Thank you for coming," I said. "It means a lot. Really."

"It's not hospital policy to attend patients' funerals but George meant a great deal to me." She smiled. "He was a difficult bugger most of the time, but every now and then I'd catch a glimpse of the man he used to be. Still was, in fact. The brother you remember. He was just buried under whatever it was that happened to him."

After that it was business as usual. George's coffin on the catafalque, surrounded by the flowers that I had provided. There was a wreath from the hospital too, and a small offering from Virginia. The minister said some words about George based on a conversation we'd had earlier the in the week. I could feel them pricking at my eyes. Somewhere, buried under the weight of the years, was the memory of the brother I knew, who'd told me stories and sometimes drifted away in odd reveries after that night in Glastonbury. I'd loved him once in that way that younger brothers do, but the years and the circumstances had parted us in some strange unknowable way. I never really saw the brother I knew once he was returned to us, the one that

Virginia would glimpse from time to time. It was just a matter of bad timing, I suppose. Even when I found him out in the hospital grounds, listening to the wireless, he was hazy around the edges, like a sepia photograph. Like a replica of the brother I'd had, replaced by someone who had a rough description of who he used to be before he went missing. It wasn't sufficient. Neither I nor my parents could find enough to hold onto, although we did. Of course we did.

After the committal, they played Fleetwood Mac's 'A Man of the World,' which was what broke me; I had to press my hand to my face and stand very still until the emotions subsided. I felt Virginia's gloved hand against my back. After a moment I opened my eyes and the coffin was almost gone, disappearing behind the curtain like some elaborate magician's trick.

There wasn't much more after that. I was told I could collect George's ashes in a couple of days. We went back outside, into the bitter cold, and Virginia and I stood in the carpark with our breath misting in the air between us.

"Do you know anything about the videotape that was in the box of his belongings?" I asked. "'Perfidious Albion.'"

"He mentioned it every now and then." Virginia considered for a moment. "He said it was all that was left. He made it, didn't he? Your dad told me that George used to work for the BBC."

"He was... well, he was *gifted*," I said. "*Ten times* smarter than all of us put together. Somehow those genes managed to skip right past me."

Virginia smiled.

"There were no other tapes?"

She shook her head. "No, that was everything."

"He never mentioned anything else about the play to you?"

"Not that I recall. I was reluctant to get him to speak about the past, to be honest. Whatever happened to George, it was too much like a minefield. Remembering something from that time could set him back. It was best to try to keep him tethered to the present as much as we could."

"He didn't have any visitors?" I asked. "Apart from Mum and Dad and myself."

After a moments consideration, she said. "There was this woman, now I think about it. She visited just once as far as I can remember."

"When was this?"

She puffed out her cheeks. "It must be about twenty years ago, I think. Yes, 1999. We were all worried about the Millennium Bug weren't we?"

"No idea who she was?"

"I can't recall her name. An old friend, I think she said. I remember she sat with him outside for an hour or so. She was dressed in really hippy-style clothes. I don't think George was very responsive that day and she was left quite upset. Do you think it's important?"

"I don't know if it is, to be honest," I admitted.

"Just don't get lost down that rabbit-hole," Virginia said, taking my hands one final time. "George never came out of it, and I'd hate for it to happen again."

~ 5 ~

I spent some time on the internet that night, looking for a thread to pull at 'Perfidious Albion'. As a *Play for Today* it had some historical interest to enthusiasts of quality golden-age British television. There was a mention of it on Wikipedia, and a couple of scholarly essays that mentioned it in passing, but by all accounts the episode was lost and so details remained, at best, oddly elusive. By the early 1970s television companies were finding it harder to justify the expense required to store much of the material they held in their libraries. Warehouses became overcrowded and a fire hazard. The BBC made the decision to destroy any film over a three-year limit that was deemed to be of little or no historical value. Subsequently episodes of shows today regarded as 'classics' such as Steptoe and Son, Hancock's Half-Hour, Dad's Army and Doctor Who were purged from the archives over a six-year period.

It was a frustrating few hours until I found a website that looked antiquated by modern standards. From what I could gather (and it took some work, clicking on various boxes and being taken to pages that no longer existed) the owner of the website, Tommy Chaplin, was a collector of rare or lost, mostly British, TV shows. There was a short listing for 'Perfidious Albion,' transmitted in 1979, listed as 'exists only as a domestic recording.' No evidence that the webpages had been maintained in some time. I scrolled to the bottom of the Home page and found an email address for Tommy Chaplin, hoping that that he was still alive and still retained an interest in old TV shows.

By the time I woke the next morning Chaplin had responded. He insisted he didn't trade in TV shows anymore, and didn't much trust anyone whom he couldn't meet first. There was some bad blood between old dealers of vintage TV shows and memorabilia. If I wanted to talk about 'Perfidious Albion' or anything TV-related I'd have to go to him.

He was a three-hour car journey away, in Hay-on-Wye. I could be there by lunch time.

The rain chased me all the way over the border into Wales and only subsided by the time I'd taken a circuit of the sleepy little town in order to find a suitable carpark. Despite the inclement weather there was still a scattering of tourists in waterproofs and stout hiking boots. They were making their way from one crowded bookstore to the next, just long enough to add to the condensation on all the windows and stare vacantly at all the tightly packed shelves. Then they would troop out and pick at unfamiliar meals at a vegan cafe before they went home, weighed down with tatty paperbacks that they probably didn't really need.

Tommy Chaplin lived in a narrow house a five-minute walk away from the town. His front door opened almost directly onto the road, which was why I couldn't park outside his house. He filled the doorway and scrutinised me with a squint that seemed to draw all his features into the middle of his face. He didn't ask who I was, which suggested that he didn't get many unfamiliar visitors. The remains of his hair was combed over his scalp with what looked like bryl-cream. He could have been anywhere between the ages of 40 and 60. After I'd introduced myself he retreated back into the gloom of his cramped hallway. I closed the door and followed him, pausing to glance at the lopsided clutter of literally hundreds of framed black and white portraits of stars of the British stage and screen. They carried over into the front room, covering every available inch of wall space, most of them faded with the sun. There were books and old-time magazines with titles like Photoplay, Continental Film Review and Film Fun putting strain on the cheap shelving units, and in piles across the threadbare carpet.

An old 40-inch cathode-ray tube TV took up a substantial piece of real estate in one corner of the room, with old VHS videotapes and DVDs stacked up on either side. Everything was coated in a thick layer of dust. Everything smelled of take-out food and cigarette ash.

"You'll have to excuse the mess," Chaplin said, rooting through the piles of shit on either side of us, and I almost laughed.

"Maid's day off," I offered, but he didn't smile.

"So. 'Perfidious Albion,'" he said.

"Yes."

"Like I said in the email, I don't release my tapes to anyone anymore. Don't trade with dealers, don't even go to the memorabilia fairs anymore, to be honest," he said, folding his arms and turning to face me. "Bunch of ruddy sharks, they are."

"I didn't realise that the tape-sharing world was such a cut-throat affair."

"You taking the Michael?"

"Not especially," I said.

He considered me with a narrowed gaze, as if trying to sniff out some kind of espionage on my part. "I've got several tapes of various *Play for*

Today episodes, and one of them is definitely this 'Perfidious Albion,'" he said finally. "It's a domestic recording, so it's a bit ropey, quality-wise. Right bleeding weird it is too. No wonder the Beeb 'lost' it."

Chaplin led me through to the back room of his narrow little home, where his collection had grown like weeds across the carpet and up the walls and everywhere in between. He picked his way through the towers of tapes and DVDs to where an ancient Mac sat on a desk in the corner. He picked up the tape that was sitting there, along with a magazine, and then turned, realised I was right behind him and there followed the absurd ballet of us turning and retracing our steps without knocking any of the towers of crap over.

"What's your interest in it, anyway?" Chaplin asked when we found our way back in the front room.

"My brother wrote and directed it."

Tommy Chaplin reconsidered me for a moment. He was weighing up what this knowledge was worth. But then the air seemed to go out of him. I think he'd suddenly realised that in burning his bridges with the memorabilia community, he'd lost any reason to horde some gem of new light cast on an old TV show. And even then, my brother's play was so obscure that it barely merited consideration for long.

"Where did you get this tape from?" I asked as Chaplin set about clearing some space on the shabby couch in front of his TV.

He tapped the side of his nose as if it was the very definition of clandestine, and then switched on the TV and slipped the tape into the dusty video recorder. "Dealer in Wolverhampton," he said finally. "Had to drive up there to get them. House clearance after this old geezer popped his clogs. He was one of those hoarder types like you see on telly. They found a room of old VHS tapes he'd made himself or bought from other dealers. I had the lot for £500." He sat down heavily on the couch and then shuffled across to make room for me. "Found a small stack of *Play for Today* episodes amongst them."

I sat down and the couch seemed to push us both together. There were hard toast crumbs like little shards of glass wherever I placed my hands. Chaplin got back up to close the curtains and then sat back down again, squinting at the remote control with his teeth bared, a loose strand of hair falling in front of his eyes. Finally the screen lit up and the video made a clattering noise as it began. Chaplin sat back and began to bite at his dirty fingernails. I remained on the edge of the couch so that we weren't sitting in each other's laps.

It came back to me as I sat in that narrow house. Gradually everything fell away: Chaplin, the room and its contents, the world beyond. Here it all was, like remembering a dream.

After following Joseph of Arimathea to Somerset's flooded land we are introduced to an awkward teenage boy, in love with an antiquated, delusory Englishness – Blake, the Church, Avalon. Over the course of the play he discovers a new identity, new desires; his prejudices are stripped away, one by one. Britain is in the midst of change; the economic 'winter of discontent', the imminent election of Margaret Thatcher. The boy runs away from his deeply religious home and finds himself sleeping in the grounds of Glastonbury Abbey. He wakes up shivering in the night with a strange otherworldly boy on his chest. "Go to sleep," he says, "I'll look after you." Another crude animation takes over, the waters rising and enveloping the abbey, the town, washing all the way to the foot of Glastonbury Tor. The isle of glass. Time becomes elastic, fluid. The faerie boy tells the runaway that all existence in time is equally real. "Everything from the past exists right now, as do things from the future; they are just not present. Do you see?" The play seems to unmoor itself for a moment and becomes a roll of celluloid stock with the images of the two boys together, the individual frames fixed. As the beam of a projector plays through the static images, the illusion of movement, of life happening, occurs. "Every moment is eternal," the boy says as the land transforms below the Tor. Saxons invade and conquer Somerset. Their king puts up a stone church, which forms the west-end of the nave of Glastonbury Abbey. The hawthorn tree flowers twice a year until the Puritans chop it down during the English Civil War. Joseph dies at the age of 86, and his body is carried by six kings in a funeral procession. The world opens up for the boy. Blake's *Jerusalem* roars. Soundbites from the Conservative election campaign drift in and out. Finally the boy turns away from it all.

There was a cumulative effect to the show that I couldn't entirely pinpoint. It was something to do with the oddly disconnected dialogue, the strange cadences, the analogue hiss in between that sounded to me like dust drifting all the way from the seventies and eighties, covering me with its strange melancholy. It was hard to know where to begin finding my way into the density of my brother's play, and that lost part of his life. I heard Chaplin tutting from very far away. I reluctantly turned to his voice.

"Nonsense," he said. "Bloody lefty shit."

"Did you understand it?" I asked.

"He was *your* brother. I was hoping you might tell me what it's all about. Why don't you ask him?"

"He's dead."

"Oh," Chaplin said. It took the wind out of his sails momentarily. "Sorry to hear that." After a moment he said, "Was it to do with them shady characters he was involved with?"

"Shady characters?"

Chaplin picked at his fingernails. "Rumour was he was involved in a cult of some kind."

"A cult? That sounds ridiculous."

Chaplin shrugged. "Don't shoot the messenger, mate. That was the rumour."

"What kind of cult?"

Chaplin shrugged again. "Who knows. Did you never think to ask him? I mean they're all going to be a loony lot if they're a cult, aren't they?"

He bundled me out of the door not long after that, but not before I'd cajoled him into using his ancient printer to photocopy the article about 'Perfidious Albion' from a tatty issue of TV Zone from 1992. Afterwards I wandered around Hay-on-Wye for a while, in and out of little bookshops, half expecting to feel the world come unmoored around me. I was hearing a phrase in my mind, repeating. It followed me on the journey home until I had to pull over and write it down on my phone. It didn't make much sense to me then, but I kept returning to it, nagging at it, trying to remember where it came from.

The persistent illusion of transience. I Googled it when I got home. It was attributed to Einstein. It was a question of physics and metaphysics. I was too tired to fall down that particular rabbit-hole. I went to bed.

The magazine article that I had Chaplin photocopy for me provided only one useful piece of information. There was a box out devoted to George's play, 'Perfidious Albion' being one of the handful of more obscure entries in the *Play for Today* run. Aside from pointing out how young and inexperienced its writer and director was during the production, there was a still from the play of the actors who'd played the boy's parents; the father, credited simply as Aesop, and the mother, credited as Charity Fairhurst.

I hadn't recognised Aesop from that solitary meeting in Glastonbury all those years ago but the more I considered it, the more I could see that it was certainly that charismatic chancer who'd fed my brother LSD. I couldn't find anything about him online, but I had more luck with Charity. I found her working for, of all things, a charity. But there seemed to be some mileage in Chaplin's claim that my brother had been involved in a cult of some kind. Charity worked for the Cult Information Group (CIG), a support organisation for victims of cults. Members of the charity gave educational talks to schools and universities, churches and corporations, and consulted with police and social agencies. Charity's name was uncommon, and the fact that she was working for this organisation only emphasised that this must be the same woman who'd been involved with my brother all those years ago. I felt that there was a good chance that Charity Fairhurst was also the woman dressed in hippy-style clothes, who'd visited George in 1999. I used the organisation's contact email to get in touch with her.

I collected George's ashes and brought the plastic urn back to the family home and stared at it. I had no idea where those ashes should reside; whether I should keep them or scatter them somewhere suitable. I rattled around the largely empty house and ended up sitting in George's room, which remained as it was all those years ago, untouched. After they found him wandering on a lonely B-road in 1988, they'd had George sectioned, but then within three or four months he was released back into my parents' care. He returned to his old bedroom and stayed there until my mother died in 1993. Early on my brother sometimes had good days where he was wholly communicative and able to look after himself.

But quite often he became restless and frustrated, almost certainly exacerbated by being sequestered in the family home, sitting down to dinner at the old table, forced to close the door and hide away in his bedroom for privacy. I visited as often as I was able but I could see the strain on my parents' faces – it just wasn't working. The son they'd longed to have returned to them had answered their prayers and finally come home, but he wasn't the George they remembered. This man was mute one day and raging with anger the next. They tried their best; of course they did. He was still their little boy, in many ways more helpless than he'd ever been as a child. They doted on him on his good days, and despaired during the bad ones. But the strain inevitably took its toll. The day after we buried my mum, my old man sat down with me and placed his hands on the kitchen table and said he couldn't cope anymore. It didn't matter how much he loved George, he was too much to handle alone. Would I help him look for somewhere suitable, somewhere close so that he could visit him? I hadn't so much as touched my old man in years, but I reached across the table and closed my hands over his and said yes, of course I would.

Charity emailed that evening and agreed to meet me. I should have left it alone. But I'd found out that George had somehow gotten involved with a cult of some kind, and that Aesop had had a larger presence in his life than I'd ever given thought to.

The old man would have wanted me to see it through, to understand what it was that had left his son like a shadow of the man he should have been. And I felt some connection to 'Perfidious Albion'. It belonged to me somehow. Part of its story had happened to me too.

~ 7 ~

I drove to London the next day and met Charity in an anonymous office building on the Seven Sisters Road near Finsbury Park. I had to buzz an intercom outside some gates to the property, a grand old Georgian building with a peeling facade. The woman who met me was wholly unlike the picture I'd formed in my head. Charity Fairhurst had bright blue eyes, short dark hair which was streaked with grey, elegantly applied make-up and nails, and wore a trouser suit and a wedding band.

"Oh, you look *so* much like your brother," was the first thing she said. "It's positively *uncanny*." She sighed and took my hands, squeezed them. "I'm *so* sorry for your loss."

She led me into a modest conference room with a long table that seated eight. There was a large TV screen at one end and some plants to soften the harshness of the room. The light fell in oblique strips across the desk. Charity sat at the end of the table and I sat down next to her.

"I wish I had known," she said. "I would have attended the funeral."

"I didn't know who you were until yesterday," I said. "Otherwise I would have contacted you."

"I visited George," she said. "Many years ago. At the hospital. But he was more or less unresponsive. The nurse did say he was having a bad day. I don't know if they just said that to make me feel better."

"His good days were few and far between."

"I didn't want to talk about, well, *him*. Aesop. I take it that's why you're here. Him. I didn't wish to rake over old ground in case it upset him. But that was what brought us together, for better or worse."

"Until a couple of days ago I didn't even know

George had been involved with a cult," I said. "That's why I'm here. He just sort of disappeared after he made his play. He stayed in touch with the odd phone call or postcard, but we didn't really know what had happened to him."

Charity nodded. "You know, once all I wanted to do was put that whole thing behind me. When I got away from Aesop I ran far away. And I mean, *really far*. I went to live alone in New Zealand. I didn't understand what had happened to me any more than George did. I stayed away for so many years, terrified of that man and what he'd done to me, to *all* of us." She sighed. "But of course, you can't run away from your life, can you? You *have* to take responsibility for it eventually."

"I met Aesop when George and I were still young," I said. "He just seemed ridiculous to me. He was like Gandhi with a bong."

Charity laughed. "He was much more than that, unfortunately. I met Aesop a couple of years after my parents died. I was homeless and sleeping on friends' sofas or in shelters. He caught me at my lowest ebb. That's how he found most of us. When we were at our most vulnerable. He offered me a place to stay, free of charge. For a while he didn't seem to want anything from me. There were other people at the flat in Glastonbury, but he seemed to be in charge somehow. That was immediately apparent. He called it a commune. To be honest I didn't care what it was at the time. He provided shelter and food and sympathy. I didn't really notice until later that the other squatters were in thrall to him.

"But then, late one evening he started asking me about my life. I responded because I wanted someone to listen to me. You know? Just to properly *listen* for once. I wanted someone to tell me that things would get better. And of course, I told him *all sorts* of things. You see, this was part of the conditioning. First he would put you at ease and make you feel like a member of the group. Next he would get you to tell him your life's story. Secrets that you'd never told anyone else. He had this mesmeric quality about him. You'd smoke a bit of blow and you would tell him things you could hardly admit to yourself. Then gradually he would take some of your creature comforts away from you. At that point I couldn't even consider leaving. Aesop had provided this home for me, acceptance, counselling even. So I was broken down, physically and mentally, until I became vulnerable to all of his suggestions. It took about three or four days, this process. And its *was* a process. At the end of it you'd have a sudden personality change. They call it 'snapping'. It leaves you unable to reason or critically evaluate. Aesop told me that every adult has secrets that they pack away deep inside themselves, as if they might be able to forget them somehow. Secret reserves of shame and regret. But of course secrets have power in the wrong hands. And believe me, he was the *wrong* hands. After that it was just this tawdry business of dominance and sex. Control. He'd routinely sexually abuse the men and women in the commune, then physically beat them and make the rest of us watch. And we would. Without a raised voice." She paused a moment. Even half a lifetime's distance didn't seem like enough, but then she gathered herself and continued.

"After that I was tasked with recruiting others and soliciting funds however I could. That was how I met George. Aesop said he knew him, and got us invited to a BBC party at Television Centre. A girl at the commune did my hair. It didn't go well initially. Aesop thought he'd fit right in with all the celebrities and executives but they seemed to look right through him. He was so livid with anger he left early. I stayed, and that night I got to know George. Even through my fogged mind I could see something pure in him. *Something good.* We talked and we had a few drinks. I was deeply attracted to him. He was a handsome boy, your brother. And he had *such* a gentle nature. He told me stories about you and your family and how he'd written some scripts for the BBC, which he was hoping to get made soon. He was so sweet and part of me wanted to resist letting Aesop get his claws into him, but then the scared, selfish part of me insisted that things would be easier if there was someone there who made me feel a little bit like the girl I used to be.

"Aesop insisted that I meet him every night for a couple of weeks before I took George back to Glastonbury. And even though I don't think he had an interest in me sexually, at that point I think I could have asked your brother to jump off a cliff with me and he would have." Charity glanced at me and then away. "I want you to know that I'm ashamed of myself for that, for my part in ruining your brother's life."

"You were young and you were vulnerable," I said. "You weren't responsible."

She nodded but I could see a distance in her eyes now, the great gulf travelled to take her back to that young girl she had been and who she never wished to be again.

"So George was still working at the BBC when he moved to Glastonbury?"

"For a while, yes. He had a good relationship with one of the producers who'd kind of adopted him. I think they were lovers for a while. George had a very childlike manner, quite guileless in a way. But people *wanted* to help him. They *wanted* to hear his ideas. And so Malcolm, this producer, packed him off to Birmingham to make his play.

"But by this time Aesop had gotten his claws into George. It doesn't matter what background you're from. He snapped George quite quickly. I think George just wanted to belong to something. I think we all did. That was Aesop's great gift, I suppose. Even after all the abuse."

"And Aesop was involved with the filming of the show?"

"He was. He insisted on adding some elements to George's script and then we went with him to Birmingham and stayed with him.

We had brief roles in it, but we weren't actors and anyway, I think the production crew got tired of Aesop. He seemed like such a little man surrounded by normal people. Like a magician who's forgotten how all his tricks work. They had him kicked off the set, so we came back to Glastonbury. He was humiliated. But then Aesop decided 'Perfidious Albion' had been a temporary distraction from what he insisted was his 'higher purpose.'"

"And what was that?"

"Well, here it is. I know how it'll sound and I shouldn't blame you if you call me mad. But this was what he made of our lives. He called it a magical event. He would carry around a tatty copy of *Slaughterhouse 5* and talk about Eternalism. Do you know what that is?"

"Not really."

"It takes the view that all existence in time is equally real. Everything from the past exists right now, as do things from the future; they're just not present."

"'The persistent illusion of transience.'" I said.

"Yes, well that was Einstein. 'The distinction between the past, present and future is only a stubbornly persistent illusion.'"

"What did Aesop want to do with the theory?"

"He believed that a magical working would unseat his consciousness in time. Sometimes when he was stoned he'd talk about someone called Emily. None of us learned who she was. He wouldn't explain. But *everything* was for Emily. Clearly something had happened to her during his life and he wanted to rescue her. But if this theory of block time was true, then that was impossible. I think he decided that even *that* could be defied by sheer force of will. We began to use psilocybin mushrooms to achieve what Aesop called a 'superior spiritual state.'"

"I suppose George was involved in all of this?"

"Yes. After the play he sort of fell through the cracks of the BBC and he eventually found his way back to us in Glastonbury. He thought Aesop had all the answers then."

"And I take it none of this ended well for anyone?"

"We spent a couple of years in that awful flat above a taxidermist's in Glastonbury. Days on end, high as kites while Aesop perfected this magical working. To this day I don't know if what he insisted was happening was the truth of things or not. But the idea that we could become unseated in time and open the door to any moment of our lives was so seductive that we all believed it. We all *wanted* to believe it. For so many years afterwards I'd forgotten almost everything about that period of my life, but it's gradually come back to me. Sometimes I can remember with incredible clarity these workings and the feeling that my consciousness had come undone somehow. I'd find myself revisiting the night I lost my virginity in the backseat of my first boyfriend's car in a lay-by in Cardiff. Or running out into the garden where my mum and dad were both sitting. The first flush of spring. Everything in bloom. My dog running around at my heels. Or going back and seeing myself being born, setting eyes on my mother for the first time. These moments, they're all so bright and perfect in my memory, as if they happened yesterday. But we couldn't remain in them for long. We would step through the door and then our consciousness couldn't stay. It drifted back to where we were, like an invisible umbilical cord.

"But Aesop kept going, kept upping our doses of various psychotropic drugs. Months and months of magical workings until it was refined.

And then there was that final rite. It unseated us all. We got lost somehow. All of us. When the police found me it was two years after that night. I had no idea where I went, no memory for years."

"You didn't try to get Aesop prosecuted?"

"You have to understand, I barely remembered anything of the time I'd spent with Aesop. I was seeing my life from all of these doorways that had opened up to me. I was sectioned for three months. Utterly out of my mind. After that it took months for me to recover to any real degree. And all I remember feeling was fear. And withdrawal from the cult. That's what it was, after all: a cult. I had months of depression and insomnia, altered states. And the absolute certainty that I had to get as far away from England as I could. It was only after several years of distance that I felt the need to come back and make some kind of real recovery. And that meant facing up to what had happened. And helping people who'd undergone similar experiences."

"What happened to the rest of the commune?"

"I tried to track them all down when I got

back. I found some of them. A lot of them were like George. They'd never recover. They barely recognised me. But they all kept trying to make their way back to that flat in Glastonbury. Like George. Some residual energy of that failed magical working, still calling out to them. That seductive urge to move through your life, in and out of doors of time and just reinhabit them again. I understand why. Even now I still dream about it. Some of them I couldn't find. I think they just vanished entirely."

"Lost in their own lives?"

"It sounds ridiculous when you say it out loud, but I *looked* for those people. They're gone. Do I think they went through a door and that door closed behind them? I can't rule it out."

"And Aesop? Do you know what happened to him?"

"Oh, yes. I made a point of tracking him down when I got back to England. Keep your enemies closer, and all that. Even though I'm married now, I'm aware every day of the shadow that odious little man has cast on my life." Charity placed her hands on the table between us. I realised that it was purely to stop them from shaking. "I went back to Glastonbury in 2002.

The building where the taxidermist was is gone. And so is the flat." She paused, looking for sense in what she was about to say. "But he's still there."

"How?"

"A few years ago I read that book Aesop used to carry around with him all the time. *Slaughterhouse 5*. Billy Pilgrim, unstuck in time." Charity's hands were shaking uncontrollably now. She reached into a handbag at her feet and took out some cigarettes. I held the lighter for her. She got up and opened a window, and immediately we were swamped with noise from the traffic on Seven Sisters Road. She exhaled the first rich plume of smoke from her lungs and leaned on the window ledge until she was steady again. "If you stand on that street," she said, "and you look hard enough I swear that you'll see that shitty taxidermist and the flat above it.

"It's still there," she said finally. "He's still there. Lost in between the cracks of time."

~ 8 ~

So I went back to Glastonbury. I hadn't visited since that day when I was 12 and George was 16.

In the intervening years Glastonbury has only become more itself. The hippies who'd existed at the fringes of the town, living in caravans and squats, barred from the pubs for their long hair and beards and chanting Hare Krishnas on the Tor during thunderstorms, are now pillars of the community, having started independent businesses, running themed guesthouses and selling incense and witchy shit. The tourist-orientated alternative. People come and go with the weather, phase of the moon and proximity of festivals.

I discovered that the fervency of my grief had been replaced with anger; I had been given a vessel into which to pour all of the feelings of iniquity and retribution, and fantasise of how I would react in the spur of the moment. It carried me across the little town with the mid-morning sun on my shoulders. I will do such things, I thought. What they are yet I know not: but they shall be the terrors of the earth.

I went looking for the area where Aesop's flat had been. Even on a crisp winter's day there was something about the quality of light in Glastonbury – everything had a faint golden cast. The shock troops of gentrification hadn't muddied their boots here yet, save for a few Grade II listed buildings on the outskirts of town. A kid in what looked like rags was chalking elaborate mandalas on the pavement. Outside St John's Church, a pale woman was playing a hang-drum. I passed a hipster-style cafe with bare Edison bulbs in the windows and artisanal coffee beans on the go. Outside there was an earnest looking thirty-something with some tasteful tattoos and a waxed moustache, sketching in his moleskine. I walked up and down the street a couple of times, drawing a blank. I knew I wouldn't see it immediately, if at all.

On my third jaunt up and down the street I could tell that the guy with the waxed moustache was getting concerned. I was spoiling his gluten-free Mochaccino brownie. Eventually he gathered up his messenger bag and fucked off. I crossed the street and waited. I tried to will into my mind my faint memory of the taxidermist's shop beneath Aesop's flat, the dusty displays of poorly stuffed owls and hares and foxes. The paint peeling from its facade. The shabby wooden staircase walk-up to Aesop's flat. I conjured it all into my third eye, closed my actual eyes and opened them again. The mandalas were flowing across the pavements, like a river had burst its banks. The hang-drum took on a ceremonial tone. A melody, repeating, never finding its resolution. I caught a fleeting glimpse and then it was gone again. I repeated the process, aware that there was an inherent sense of ritual working to it. On my fifth try the cafe got tangled in my eyelashes and then I blinked and it was gone, replaced with the past.

There was the taxidermist shop.

I crossed the street, pressed my face to the glass and peered into the shadowy interior, at the narrow counter and the glass cases of rare tarantulas and butterflies. I didn't want to relinquish my contact with the window lest time swallow it back up again and leave me hovering like a crazy in the doorway of the cafe. I glanced back down the street and for a moment it was a multitude of streets, a million moments in time all happening at once. It was a day in the 70s. I'd followed my brother all the way here only for him to lose part of his mind. A day, just like any other, to everyone but us. The notion made my gut churn and I stumbled away from it, into the doorway and up the narrow staircase to Aesop's flat.

I have no real facility for the language required to describe that approach to his doorway, and everything afterward. I felt the change within me, a static charge of energy that set my nerves on fire and my hair on end. A sense of hovering on the periphery of utter chaos; a tipping point that couldn't ever be unseen or undone. The door opened when I pressed my weight against it, and allowed me entry into a narrow corridor which, as I slipped inside it, stretched away from me, wholly elastic. I gripped the walls and stumbled down the hallway, feeling a pressure building inside my head, a forest fire of gargantuan proportions behind my eyes. I walked for hours, I think, until I reached another room. I hesitated on the precipice, aware of the disjunction between my perception of things and the actuality of them. By the time I crossed the threshold I had been swallowed by a rabbit hole wholly of Aesop's making. The poky front room was sparsely furnished but much as I recalled. Two shabby cast-off couches arranged around a inglenook fireplace blackened with soot. There was a threadbare Persian rug laid over the bare wooden boards, and an old TV and VCR in the corner of the room, tapes scattered across the floor. I could see it all as if from a great height and then through a fish-eye lens. I swam through the air with my legs kicking at nothing and arrived in the centre of the room, where I found crude symbols scored into the wooden floorboards and half-concealed by the rug. An upturned top-hat in the centre of the room that someone had used as a target to catch tarot cards. They were scattered all around it; the tower, the moon, the fool, the hierophant. My feet came to rest on the rug and my stomach followed a moment later. There was a potent scent of sage and incense in the air, alongside the staleness of a man sitting alone in a room for too long. Stale sweat and farts and desperation. I considered the VHS tapes scattered in front of the TV. British pornography, as dated as 70s sit-coms. I hesitated at the drawn curtains. As I began to raise my hands to open them I was gripped with a fear of what would be beyond the window, that Glastonbury might have been snatched away in the time it had taken me to climb that staircase and stumble down the corridor that led to this room. Then I heard a toilet flush and everything uncanny about this moment dissolved entirely. I turned around and there he was standing in the doorway, wiping his hands on his vest. I laughed – at the absurdity, and as a reaction to the relief flooding through my system. I had expected some sense of threat if and when I finally laid eyes on Aesop, but he fell far short of expectations. In this moment he was a man in his mid-seventies. He had a thick frizzy grey beard. Drawstring sweat-pants and a white, long out of shape vest. His toenails were long and curled, like talons. He had a multitude of ornate rings on his yellowed fingers. He smiled blandly at me, utterly unfazed at my presence in his front room, and sat down. He reached down the far side of the couch beside the fireplace and withdrew a crumpled Morrison's carrier bag that contained a pouch of tobacco and a lighter. He started rolling a cigarette. "Don't just stand there, like a spare part," he said. "Sit down." He glanced across at me. "Do you want a drink? Tea, coffee? The milk might be off by now. I forget when I bought it."

"No," I said.

"You're here about George," he said when he was finished with the roll-up. He sealed it with his tongue and lit it, exhaled a plume of smoke. "I remember you. Little seeker, so you are."

"If I open the curtains what will I see?" I asked.

"Glastonbury," he said. "We haven't fucking gone anywhere. Damn fool you are too."

Only his eyes seemed familiar to me. Cruel green eyes, pale and cowardly and devious. Nothing else remained of that beautiful and charismatic messiah. We talked, off and on, for an hour, or three days, or five years. I have no idea. Some of these exchanges happened sequentially, some of them happened before or after. I present them here in an order that seems at least comprehensible.

"I'm not what you were expecting," he said.

"No. You're just a man. Norman Hardinge," I said. "That's your real name, isn't it?" Charity had uncovered it when she'd returned to England. Giving him his real name had greatly reduced the shadow he'd cast over her life, she'd told me. And it did. Norman had been gifted the flat in the seventies by his father, who was one of the non-royal dukes.

He wrinkled his nose at the name, but it didn't seem to agitate him greatly.

"This place," I said. "This building. The taxidermist downstairs. It's not really here anymore, is it?"

He shrugged and the world shifted around us, a subtle Escher-like reorganisation of the rooms. Time, slipping. "Something happened. Some spectacular by-product of the magical working I performed in 1987. I couldn't properly explain it to you, to be honest."

"George is dead," I said. "He was killed in an accident, trying to make his way back here."

"Yes," Aesop said. "They all try to return at some point or another. The residual energy of that magical event seems to remain in their DNA, calling them back. Of course, we lost some of them altogether on that day. It's unfortunate."

"Unfortunate?"

"You have to understand. People are much more amenable to being told what to do than you might expect. Some people are just looking for someone to give them direction, meaning. Even if you're full of shit."

"So you're not subjugating them if they're weak-willed?"

I found myself talking with Aesop in the kitchen, where everything was out of date, where food was rotting in the bin and there were dead bluebottles lined up on the window ledge. Then we were in the bedroom beside the map of his life. Then we were both standing in the bath like a couple of loons.

"Your brother, Charity, the rest of them, they were like lost sheep. I realised I had some kind of *hold* over them." He extinguished the cigarette and ran a hand over his bald skull. "Debasement quickly follows when you're practically omnipotent. But I soon tired of fucking them and watching them fuck each other. So I began a series of workings, events if you will, with chosen members of the group. Exploratory sessions using LSD, psilocybin mushrooms."

"In order to move through time?"

He smiled. "We don't experience the universe directly. We experience through these limited senses of ours and we agree that this is reality. Whatever *that* means. Take five grams of dried psilocybin mushrooms on an empty stomach in a silent, darkened room and tell me what reality is!"

"Was it worth it," I asked. "To end up like this?"

"I don't expect you to grasp the situation, seeker," he said. "I'm not just here, I'm *everywhere*. For me, time is happening all at once. I am outside all of this. This frail shell of a body that you see before you. In just a click of my fingers I am divested of this bag of bones. I'm pure. *Fucking. Energy.* I accept it's a slippery concept to grasp. I'm merely a passenger. I wasn't schooled, I don't understand it myself. But since 1987 I am a thing best left to scientists and poets to describe. I close my eyes and millions, trillions of doors that lead to each and every moment of my life can be entered. Open any door and I am part of life's spectacular pattern again, its profoundly beautiful design.

"Open one door and I'm a little boy again in a school yard, chasing a girl called Rebecca whom I have longed to kiss for six months, one week and two days. Through another and I'm watching Father slaughter chickens in our gardens, and their headless bodies are flapping their wings and stumbling towards me, and I'm screaming blue bloody murder in fear. Open another door and I can see you trailing after your brother, wide-eyed at all the pretty girls, and getting stoned on second-hand smoke. You buggered off to sleep in my room, once you'd looked at my map."

I remember something Charity had said to me. "What about Emily?"

Whatever kind of distress he'd once carried with him, Aesop gave the impression that he was no longer in thrall to it. "Early on I thought I could rescue her from time but that was impossible. Eternalism doesn't allow for that. All of the points in space-time are fixed and unchanging. But I realised that it didn't matter. Everything, in a sense, is happening now. Every one of Emily's moments on this planet is unfolding like stars coming to life and I can be a party to every single one of them. And I have. I am. I will be. I—"

And then he was gone. I watched him dissolve into the air around me. I clambered out of the bath and returned to the front room and waited. I felt I had done this already, more than once, but Aesop had come back on those occasions. I couldn't sufficiently get a handle of the metaphysics of it. I switched on the TV and turned it back off again. I leafed through his books and glanced out of the window. It had gotten dark. It got light again. And dark. Eventually I found the dried psilocybin mushrooms in a paper bag down the side of the couch. I suppose it was inevitable. "Take five milligrams on an empty stomach in a silent darkened room and tell me what reality is," I said to the room.

In the dark I came untethered, undone. Mouth dry, heart pounding, euphoria surging through my body, but frayed with anxiety at the fringes of everything. I shook and I laughed and I cried. My vision became clearer, like my mind had wiped the world clean and finally I could see it as it really was. Colours intensified until they began to hurt my eyes. The Persian rug came to life beneath my feet, geometric patterns forming and separating on a cycle until they became fractals, disintegrating in slow motion, and then coming back together. I could see my place in the world very clearly. I could see my family, all of them alive again and together. When I looked across our kitchen table at George he was eight years old, he was twelve, he was sixteen and we were making sandwiches early in the morning to eat on the bus to Glastonbury.

I sank backwards into the fabric of the couch, deep into its folds and out the other side. It was a door, of sorts. It was night and I was at the base of Glastonbury Tor. Everything was flooded with thick pink moonlight. I could see the ragged grey tower silhouetted above me. Behind me, there was Dave the Sage, the stoner kid, leaning against his VW camper van. A Dion Fortune paperback in one hand and a spliff in the other. Through adult eyes he just seemed like a kid. He had nervous hands. *These terraces circle the Tor seven times and lead you to the entrance of Annwn, the Celtic underworld,* he'd said. *Accept the hospitality of the faeries by partaking of their food and drink and you'll never be able to leave their world again.*

I could just make out two figures on the side of the Tor, traversing the terraces, making their ponderous way through a storm to the top. They were almost there. The little kid, covered in mud and cow shit, was trailing after the bigger one, calling out his name, telling him not to get ahead of him, a note of panic rising in his voice. I remember feeling alone. I felt alone now. That was my brother up there, but at the same time he was no longer here on this Earth. He was ashes.

I could smell the fresh scent of ozone in the air as it changed around us. I began to run up the hill, rain rolling down my face, limbs so light it felt like I was flying across the chalk path towards the figures above me. Below me the world fell away, all the red roofs and spires of the ancient isle of Somerset, flooded Avalon. My breath grew ragged as the hill steepened. My shadow fell away beneath me as time stretched, became elastic in my mind. I saw all of the rivers and hills and forests, the sea haze in the distance. I heard their voices above me. I heard two children arrive at the entrance at the end of the labyrinth and the storm hold its breath. I felt all the hair prick up on the back of my neck as my 12-year old self said my brother's name so plaintively it almost broke my heart in two. I heard the sound of celebration and caught my first glimpse of the celebrants. There was music in the air. The breeze was suddenly warm and fragrant. I could almost taste their bounty on my tongue.

I could feel the *pull*.

They turned to the children then, these impossibly beautiful things, made of stardust and poets' fevered imaginations, and my knees buckled. For a moment my resolve weakened. I could see now why George had lost part of his mind here. Here was where the world had come undone and revealed itself nakedly; had offered him a place to be, somewhere away from casual cruelty and indifference. Here was where Albion had turned its back. This was why George had followed Aesop through doors into time. I could see the allure of unseating yourself and going through the door labelled Mum and Dad, or every dog you ever loved more than life. Everyone who ever went away from you, yours to sit beside and drink dry. A wish that time could not dissolve.

"George," I heard myself say. My throat was tight, clotted with all the words I knew I could not say to him. "Come away now," I said. "There's a good lad."

I took the small boy into my arms first and embraced him. It was like looking through the wrong end of a telescope. I was so far away. I held out a hand to my brother and he seemed very small, very young, wholly uncertain. At the time he'd seemed like a rock. I'd only have to swim to him to be safe in a storm, but that boy went away after this night. A little bit further every day afterward. I didn't even look at the Pale Folk. I could sense the change. Everything withering around us.

"There we are now," I said. "Come away."

George glanced back one final time and then I took hold of his arm, pulled him close too. George was shaking. I held my brother tightly until he stopped. I understood that this moment was the door I would travel through, time and time again. But I had to let it go, and so I did.

And then the world was just the world again.

~ 9 ~

I put my parents' house up for sale. The night I got back from Glastonbury, I walked around the rooms, looking at all the things that had exerted an emotional pull on me and found that somehow the hold this place had on me was now gone. A line had been drawn under the past. The pitted wooden table in the kitchen, all of George's things in his shrine of a bedroom, the furniture, the pictures, my dad's books, my mother's fossil collection; every one of those things seemed to say: *You can let go now. We've held you here long enough.*

I'd stumbled away from Aesop's flat, afraid of how much time had passed while I was up there. It was night. The moon was hiding its face. The streets were all but deserted. I hadn't trusted my phone to tell me the truth. I was still aware that everything I saw might be a hallucination of some kind. I tried to walk it off but everything was creased and coloured with what I'd seen in that flat. The dark windows of the shops were reflected with light and the things hiding behind it. I tried to call a taxi but the drugs devoured the words on my tongue. There was a sense of slow decay, eating away at the certainty of everything I witnessed. It retreated after several days but that uncertainty remains. It sits behind the sofa and just outside the window, nibbling away at whatever foundation I had within the world. Everything is the same, but tainted somehow.

I finally found a little taxi firm on Market Street, not fifty yards away from where Aesop's flat once sat. I'd wandered up and down that same narrow street in Glastonbury for hours, just another fried casualty that the residents have learned to ignore after a certain hour. I managed to give them my address, all-too aware of the buzzing of their fluorescent lights and the crackle of radios and the creaking of their leather chairs in the waiting room.

How I got from there to my parents' bed is

anyone's guess, but I woke the next day with my head feeling like a balloon. I floated downstairs and drank as much water as I could, and then sat staring blankly out of the window for what seemed like days. I couldn't decide if it was just a potent mixture of psychedelic drugs that had taken me that far away from the world, or if it was a really bad foundation of magical ritual that had tainted it all.

Was the time really out of joint? Had Aesop actually managed a crude form of temporal displacement? Did I really remember a man saving us from the Underworld buried beneath Glastonbury Tor when I was twelve? Had I resolved that circle somehow by saving myself? And if so, surely that was impossible – if I'd gone to that place in my history I could only be present; I couldn't tamper with something that was fixed and unchanging. This was the conflict that Aesop had encountered with Emily, whoever she was. Wife, sister, mother, lover: the unfinished business of life. The place in our histories where the corner of the page is turned over, so we can return to it again and again, unable to tamper with its certainty.

I took George's ashes back to Glastonbury

Tor. I didn't really want to but I couldn't think of anywhere else he'd rather be. I tried to retrace the steps we'd taken as kids, walking the labyrinth the way we had that day, a little ritual of my own that I thought my brother might appreciate. The chalk path, the pilgrims' way. But it started to get late, and a storm was approaching again. It would turn out to be a large arctic airmass, stretching from the Far East of Russia. We'd even have snowfall by the end of that week. By the time I'd reached the top the wind was howling and I'd cut some corners; there'd be no entrance to the Underworld opening up for us this time. I stood there at the top of the world, clutching a plastic urn of my brother's ashes, my teeth chattering, the wind gusting around me. As I opened the urn I saw George, sitting out in the grounds of the hospital in his bright scarf with his thick grey hair tied back in a rough ponytail, listening to the football results; I saw George doing his homework across the pitted table in our kitchen; I saw George with his car loaded up with his possessions, driving away from home, from us all; I saw George beside a vast pink moon as the world opened up and offered us its bountiful secrets. I saw it all in an instant; a lifetime of joy and sorrow and everything in between. He was my brother. I offered him back to Albion, to the storm. It took him greedily, scattered him all across the Isle of Avalon.

The storm continued until the final night at my parents' house. I was packed and ready to leave the following morning. I listened to it rage across the wild untended fields and drystone walls, across the rampaging swells of the ocean. A storm that had howled for six days straight. I woke in the night from a dream of opening doors into the future and understanding that it was all still unwritten. I went to the window, pulled back the curtains. A new day was glimmering on the horizon. The world was momentarily at peace. A magnificent stillness. The storm was gone.

Also by Simon Avery:

Novellas

The Teardrop Method (TTA Press, 2017)

*Now available and forthcoming from
Black Shuck Shadows:*

Shadows 1 – The Spirits of Christmas
by Paul Kane

Shadows 2 – Tales of New Mexico
by Joseph D'Lacey

Shadows 3 – Unquiet Waters
by Thana Niveau

Shadows 4 – The Life Cycle
by Paul Kane

Shadows 5 – The Death of Boys
by Gary Fry

Shadows 6 – Broken on the Inside
by Phil Sloman

Shadows 7 – The Martledge Variations
by Simon Kurt Unsworth

Shadows 8 – Singing Back the Dark
by Simon Bestwick

Shadows 25 – Nine Ghosts

by Simon Bestwick

Shadows 26 – Hinterlands

by George Sandison

Shadows 27 – Beyond Glass

by Rachel Knightley

Shadows 28 – A Box Full of Darkness

by Simon Avery

blackshuckbooks.co.uk/shadows